SIREN
Publishing

Ménage Everlasting

Spring
IN THE
Border Lands

Marla Monroe

MEN OF THE BORDER LANDS 16

Spring in the Border Lands

Gail is tired of being coddled. Yes, she's pregnant, but she's not an invalid. She wants her men and to do something besides sit around.

Benton and Travis are terrified that something will happen to Gail or the baby. They only want what is best for her and that doesn't mean constant sex or working in the garden. She needs rest and all the protection they can give her. Only Gail is having none of it.

Then there's the whole delivery thing that has both men on edge. Delivering their baby wasn't something they'd thought of when they'd been making the baby in the first place. Now they have to bone up on the subject and manage to lull Gail in to thinking they had it all under control.

Spring brings a new life, a change of heart, and a grizzly bear. They learn to find a way to accept each other's strengths and weaknesses in order to make spring a Border Lands success.

Genre: Futuristic, Ménage a Trois/Quatre, Science-Fiction
Length: 33,433 words

SPRING IN THE BORDER LANDS

Men of the Border Lands 16

Marla Monroe

Siren Publishing, Inc.
www.SirenPublishing.com

ABOUT THE AUTHOR

Marla Monroe has been writing professionally for over thirteen years. Her first book with Siren was published in January of 2011, and she now has over 85 books available with them. She loves to write and spends every spare minute either at the keyboard or reading. She writes everything from sizzling-hot cowboys, emotionally charged BDSM, and dangerously addictive shifters, to science fiction ménages with the occasional badass biker thrown in for good measure.

Marla lives in the southern US and works full-time at a busy hospital. When not writing, she loves to travel, spend time with her feline muses, and read. Although she misses her cross-stitch and putting together puzzles, she is much happier writing fantasy worlds where she can make everyone's dreams come true. She's always eager to try something new and thoroughly enjoys the research she does for her books. She loves to hear from readers about what they are looking for in their reading adventures.

You can reach Marla at themarlamonroe@yahoo.com, or
Visit her website at www.marlamonroe.com
Her blog: www.themarlamonroe.blogspot.com
Twitter: @MarlaMonroe1
Facebook: www.facebook.com/marla.monroe.7
Google+: https://plus.google.com/u/0/+marlamonroe7/posts
Goodreads:
https://www.goodreads.com/author/show/4562866.Marla_Monroe
Pinterest: http://www.pinterest.com/marlamonroe/
BookStrand: http://bit.ly/MzcA6I
    Amazon page: http://amzn.to/1euRooO

For all titles by Marla Monroe, please visit
www.bookstrand.com/marla-monroe

SPRING IN THE BORDER LANDS

Men of the Border Lands 16

MARLA MONROE
Copyright © 2018

Chapter One

"I swear those wolves are going to turn on us one day," Benton said.

"No they won't. They know we're their family. They'll protect us. You'll see." Gail threw the stick, and all four of the nearly adult wolves tore after it, tumbling over each other to reach it first.

As was normal, Wolfie grabbed the stick but gave it over to Sasha who'd turned out to be the Alpha female. Wolfie was her Beta. Sasha pranced her way back to drop the stick at Gail's feet.

She praised Sasha, then Wolfie. Then she rubbed Gigi and Max on the head so that they wouldn't feel left out. She loved them so much. Since she'd become pregnant they'd proven to be extra observant around her. If the men argued over anything, they circled Gail and pushed her back from them. It amused Travis, but Benton didn't like it. He was worried they'd attack them if they misunderstood their moods.

Gail had told them over and over they wouldn't. She trusted them. Maybe she was a fool for doing it, but something about the way they watched and followed orders made her believe in her heart that the wolves would die protecting them.

Though it was cold out, with her coat and thermal underwear on, she was comfortable. It was nearly April now, and the men would soon be busy planting the garden. She was due sometime in May or June. She wasn't exactly sure when. She prayed it would be May so that she would be able to take care of the baby and put up the vegetables for the next winter. Right then, she was a little afraid. The farther along she got, the more protective the men got. It worried her that they wouldn't let her work once the baby was born, and they couldn't possibly take care of the garden and put up the vegetables all alone.

"Come on, Gail. Time to go inside. You've been outside long enough." Benton wrapped his arms around her from behind with his hands over her baby bump.

Well, it was more like a baby watermelon now. She covered his hands with hers then turned in his arms.

"I'm ready. Thanks for not putting up a fight about coming outside. I'm going stir-crazy inside. This is the first day it hasn't either rained or snowed in weeks."

"I know, honey." He kissed her forehead then pulled back and led her inside.

Travis had gone hunting and would be back soon, she hoped. She always worried about the men when they were gone. She was afraid that something would happen to one of them and they wouldn't be able to find them in time. She realized that her worries and fears had gotten bigger with the advancement of her pregnancy. It had to be the mothering instinct kicking in.

"Go put your legs up, and I'll bring you some hot tea, hon."

Gail didn't argue. She'd started having some swelling in her feet and ankles the last few weeks and knew from the books they'd been reading that it was a sign of blood pressure problems as well as a normal problem with pregnancy. She wasn't going to take any chances with her baby, so she followed her men's directions and put her feet up every chance she got.

Today they weren't nearly as swollen as usual. She propped them up on the couch and waited for Benton to join her. The fire crackled in the fireplace with a stew simmering in the pot hanging on the pole to one side.

Benton walked into the living room with two cups and poured some hot water from the kettle over the makeshift tea bags they'd rigged up to hold the dandelion tea they'd dried. He handed her one and kept one cup for himself. He sat on the couch, lifting her feet onto his lap. They dipped their bags in and out of the water to disperse the flavor without talking. She liked that about Benton. He didn't feel the need for conversation, and she felt comfortable with him that way.

Travis loved to talk, so she was never without someone to talk to, but sometimes it felt good just to sit and be. The two men were so different, yet they got along fine. The few minor disagreements were never concerning her, and if they ever did have a difference of opinion concerning her, they settled it outside of her hearing.

Most of the time she enjoyed it when they tied up over something. They were so funny with their swearing and muttering when they did. It never lasted long. One of them would finally cede to the other one over the subject, and that would be the end of it.

"How are you feeling today, Gail?" Benton asked after a few minutes.

"Good. My feet aren't very swollen, and getting out in the fresh air was nice. I could probably take a nap now."

"Go ahead. I'll wake you when Travis gets back. I hope he manages to get something for tomorrow. We're nearly out of dried meat for soups and stews."

"He will. I just hope it isn't a moose." She laughed with Benton.

Every time Travis came back with a moose, they spent an entire day cleaning and cutting it up. While it was fine for the dead of winter since they could store it in their cold boxes, it wasn't cold enough to freeze now, so much of the meat would go bad before they could eat it. Though they had solar energy running the fridge, there wasn't enough room in the freezer for much. Even with the wolves, some of it wouldn't get eaten. That meant they had to take it out far enough away from the house to dispose of it so that other wild animals didn't stumble on their home.

"Tell me about it. If he does that, he's going to drag the damn thing back to where he killed it."

Gail sighed and snuggled down against the pillow on the couch and closed her eyes. She immediately felt the wolves gather around her end of the couch. She smiled. They were her personal bodyguards. She had a whole entourage of them. Between them and Travis and Benton, Gail didn't think she ever had to worry about anything again.

* * * *

Travis sighed when he could see the cabin ahead of him. The deer weighed a thousand pounds at least, he decided. Dragging it from where it had finally fallen had put him quite a ways from the house. The little sled they'd made for that purpose had come in handy, but it had still been a chore. He was never so glad to see the place as right then.

He started toward the house, and the door opened. Benton walked out to meet him.

"I guess the wolves told you I was here," Travis said.

"Yep. Wolfie stood up and whined in the direction of the door." Benton helped him with the sled.

They hung the deer on the hook over the tree limb then went inside to gather the knives and pans to process the deer. Benton took Travis's out of his hands and nodded toward the living room.

"Go wake Gail and let her know that you're home. She worries when we're gone. I promised I'd wake her up when you got back."

Travis nodded. "I'll be out in a few minutes to help."

He walked into the living room to find Gail sound asleep on the couch. The wolves were lying around the floor in front of the couch and lifted their heads to peer at him before lowering their heads to doze. Travis eased between them to reach Gail's head and kissed her on the cheek.

"Hey, sleepyhead. I'm home."

Her eyelids fluttered open, and she smiled, reaching up to encircle his neck. "Hey, you. Did you kill anything?"

"Got a deer. We're going to process it now," he said.

"I need to get up and help." She started to sit up, but Travis held her down.

"No need. It's a small deer so it won't take long, and we'll take care of it tonight. You can dry some of it tomorrow. No need for you to get up yet. Rest, babe."

"I hate for you guys to do all the work. There's nothing wrong with me that I can't help you."

"I know, but we've got this. Like I said, it wasn't a big one. There'll be enough for the wolves for a couple of days and plenty for us. We'll have deer steak tomorrow and enough for stew for a few days depending on how much there is for you to dry in the dehydrator."

"I can put some up in jars if there's enough left," she said.

"We'll see. Go on back to sleep, babe. I'll wake you up when we come inside."

"Are you sure?" Gail asked.

"I'm sure." He made sure she lay back down then returned to the kitchen to grab another couple of pans.

"How'd you convince her not to get up and help us?" Benton asked.

"Told her it was a small deer and there wouldn't be a lot to mess with."

"Liar. This thing's nearly as big as a damn moose."

"Yeah, tell me about it. I nearly let it pass but was tired of sitting out there in the cold. Plus, I dragged the damn thing nearly four miles to get back home. I know exactly how big it is."

Travis worked on skinning the hide while Benton gutted it using the largest dish pan they had to catch the blood. They didn't want any to splash on the ground and alert any predators. It took them a good three hours to finish up with the deer. While Travis carried the meat inside, Benton cut the deer down and used the sled to drag it away from the house as far as he could and returned to help with cooking the meat.

They fed the wolves outside then called them back in after an hour. They immediately returned to guard their mistress while the men worked on the meat. Travis had to admit that they were well behaved for wolves. Most dogs wouldn't ignore what was going on in the kitchen like they were.

They cut up three nice-sized steaks, wrapped them in cheesecloth, then stored them in the fridge. They did the same with as much of the meat as they could fit in the freezer. Then they cut thin strips of the meat and layered them in a covered pot for Gail to put in the dehydrator the next day. The rest they stored in the fridge for the wolves.

Travis washed up then went to wake Gail again. He was sure she had to be starved. It had been a long time since she would have had lunch. He'd had some deer jerky while he'd been out, so he was just as hungry.

"Ready for some stew, babe?" he asked when she opened her eyes.

"Mmm. I can't wait. It's been simmering over there making my mouth water all day," she told him.

Benton walked in with three bowls and spoons. "We're out of bread again. It's going to be just stew tonight," he said.

"I'll make some more flatbread tomorrow while the dehydrator is going." Gail licked her lips when Benton handed her a bowl full of stew.

She smiled at him. Travis knew that Benton had made sure he'd given her extra meat. She needed it more than they did. She was eating for two now. Being sure she didn't go without was of the utmost importance to him and Travis.

"How much of the deer were you able to freeze?" she asked.

"Filled the freezer back up and have plenty in the fridge with plenty for the wolves and a steak a piece for us tomorrow," Travis said.

"Did you have any left over?" she asked.

"Nope. We fed the wolves then dragged the carcass away and emptied the blood near the stream. The deer was just the right size," Benton said.

When Gail handed her empty bowl to Travis, he asked if she wanted more.

"No thanks. I might want a snack before bed, but I'm full right now."

Travis walked over to the fire, added a log, and, using a pot holder, carried the rest of the stew back into the kitchen where he stored what there was left in a covered dish and squeezed it into the fridge. There was some dried fruit left that he'd fix for her later.

While he was in the kitchen, Benton followed him in with their bowls. He washed and Travis dried. They'd taken up some of Gail's normal chores to keep her off her feet. Though they didn't think she had that pre-eclampsia that was talked about in the books they'd read, they weren't taking any chances.

Travis was thankful she hadn't balked about staying off her feet and resting more. All in all, Gail had been easy to live with despite the pregnancy hormones that had her growling one minute and crying the next. At first it had upset them, but they'd quickly gotten used to the wild mood swings.

I'm just happy she appears to be healthy. I can handle the attitude and weeping.

Benton seemed to worry the most out of the three of them. He didn't want her to be alone in the house at any time, but when they cleaned the deer and when they started the garden once the weather warmed up, she'd be inside alone. He wasn't sure how the other man would handle it.

He decided that when the weather was nice, she could sit out on the porch and watch them. That way they would be able to keep an eye on her. Plus, the fresh air would be good for her and the baby.

The closer her due time came, the antsier he felt about delivering her baby. They'd read up on the process more than once and probably would again every few weeks, but reading about it and doing it were two different things. He'd delivered calves before and had been around dogs when they gave birth, but never a human. Hell, he hadn't even been at the hospital when his mom had had his younger brother. That had been so long ago he'd nearly forgotten about it. He'd been ten at the time. Not long after that everything had changed with the disasters and diseases that had followed. Everyone in his family had perished one way or another. He'd taken care of his younger brother until he'd fallen ill and died. After that he'd been on his own.

It hadn't been easy surviving at that age. He'd been a mere child really, but had grown up fast. For the first few years he'd run with a gang of boys his age and older, then when they'd started hurting people for their food and supplies, he'd left them and made his way west. That was where he'd met up with Benton and the two had become fast friends.

Now they had a woman. Their perfect woman, and she was giving them a child to raise. It wouldn't be easy, but they'd make it just fine. All they had to do was watch over them and provide for them. Surely with two of them they could manage that.

Chapter Two

Gail woke the next morning to find that neither man was awake. She smiled. It wasn't often that she got to watch them sleep. Normally they were up before her. Travis had one arm over her waist and faced back while Benton was turned the other way. She had her arm around him and relished the feel of his warm flesh beneath her hand. She contemplated tickling him but decided to kiss him awake instead.

"Mmm, morning, hon. What a way to wake up." Benton's deep voice, raspy from sleep sounded wonderful to her.

"I slept great. I'm hungry though and need to pee."

"I'll move so you can get up." He sat up on the side of the bed and helped her climb off.

"Where you going, babe?" Travis yawned, releasing his hold on her.

"Bathroom," she said.

"Hmm. Hurry back. It's cold without you," Travis said.

"I'm going downstairs to get something to eat. I'm hungry."

"You and that baby are always hungry," Travis teased. "I'll go fix you something for breakfast while you get dressed."

Gail didn't waste time. She needed to pee something awful. Another condition of her pregnancy was that the baby was sitting on her bladder and had no mercy. After she'd cleaned up, Gail pulled on a pair of oversized sweatpants and long-sleeved shirt. The material strained over her now enormous breasts. Those the guys were most proud of, she'd found out. It made her smile at how they'd taken great enjoyment playing with them.

When she got downstairs, Tavis had a small steak cooked over the open fire with a side of potatoes. They were only cooking them for her since there were only a few cans of them left. She couldn't wait until they started getting fresh vegetables out of the garden. It wouldn't be easy work, but it would be necessary to keep them alive during the winter. They couldn't depend on killing deer and such all winter.

"Here you go, babe. Grilled just like you like it." Travis set the plate in front of her while he and Benton sat down with their one plate, minus the potatoes.

She didn't comment on the fact they didn't share the potatoes. They'd put an end to that conversation the first time she'd brought it up. She had to think of the baby, and they'd be fine without them for now.

I love them so much. They think about me before themselves. Always. I'm so damn lucky to have stumbled on them like I did.

"What's on the agenda today for you guys?" she asked.

"I'm going to work on tanning the skins we have. They'll make good baby blankets once they're ready. The rabbit skin is perfect for one. The deer will be good for nights," Travis said.

"I'm working in the cellar some today," Benton told her. "I want to clean it out in preparation for the root vegetables we'll grow, and I want to rearrange the jars and cans we have left so that they're on the lower shelves. We'll want to use them first before we use the new ones we put up."

"I'll handle the deer strips with the dehydrator. Were you able to get many?" she asked.

"Enough for two runs, I think, hon." Benton moved the gadget closer to the counter so that she could easily reach it over her protruding stomach. "Remember to put up your feet in between."

"I will. Sure wish I had something to do while I'm sitting on the couch," she told them.

"Keep thinking of baby names. We haven't settled on any yet." Travis stood and raked off his plate in their scraps can before taking Benton's from him.

"Leave the dishes. I'll do them." Gail finished her own meal and stood up.

"As long as you promise not to overdo it today. I'll be right downstairs. All you have to do is holler for me. Don't come down those stairs for any reason, honey. I'm afraid you'll get overbalanced and fall." Benton kissed the top of her head.

"I won't. Maybe I'll work with the wolves some, and see if I can teach them to get help for me if I need it," she said.

"I have a feeling you don't need to teach them that little trick," Trenton said. "They are so damn protective of you we don't dare make you mad."

Benton nodded. "I'm still worried they'll attack one of us if they think we're hurting you."

"I keep telling you they won't. They like you guys, too," she said.

"I agree with her, Benton. I really don't think they'll attack us." Travis ruffled Gail's hair then kissed her on the cheek. "Have a good time while I'm outside. I'll check on you in a little while."

Once both men had gone their separate ways, Gail took her plate to the sink and washed everything up. Then she got the strips of deer meat from the fridge, arranged them in the dehydrator, and turned it on. She replaced the remainder of the meat in the refrigerator. All she could do now was sit on the couch with her feet up. Gail was really getting tired of that. She wanted to do something useful. Then it hit her. She could use some of the clothes that wouldn't fit any of them but that they kept in the back bedroom to create a few baby things until they could go down to town to raid the store one last time.

Gail pushed herself off the sofa and made her way carefully up the stairs. She sifted through the clothes for the softest things, which turned out to be pajamas and thermal underwear. She threw the items over her shoulder then pulled out the sewing basket she'd found when they'd gone through the rooms and headed back downstairs. Going down with the basket proved to be more difficult than she'd expected, but she managed to get to the bottom without incident. The men were going to have a fit when they realized what she'd done.

The wolves had followed her every step of the way but had kept out of her way. They seemed to know she was doing something she shouldn't have since they whined at her the entire trip up and down the stairs.

Gail carried everything into the kitchen and used the table to lay out the first set of pajamas. She couldn't help but smile that she'd be creating something for her baby by her own hands. The soft material would be perfect for a onesie. She estimated the size she needed to make it and carefully cut it out, so that the material looked like a letter small letter "t" with a curved neck at the top.

She stopped to check on the meat in the dehydrator. Another hour and they'd be ready to take up. It only took about four hours with the dehydrator until the meat was perfect for munching on and using to flavor stews and soups.

I can't wait to see my baby in one of these outfits I'm making. I just hope they fit.

Since it had been years since she'd even seen a baby, Gail wasn't sure if she remembered the right size. The youngest child back at the farm where she'd been living had been four. There had been a few of the women pregnant, but none had given birth before she'd been abducted.

She threaded a needle and began the arduous task of hand sewing the outfit together. She made tiny stitches close together so the outfit would withstand the harsh hand washing they were forced to do since they didn't have enough electricity for the washing machine and dryer. She'd just finished one side when Benton stomped up the stairs from the cellar and walked into the room.

"Hey, hon. What are you doing?"

"I decided I needed to make some outfits for the baby." She held up the one she was working on.

"Where did you get all of that?" he asked.

"From the spare bedroom where all the extra clothes are. I picked out the softest material I could."

"You went up and down the stairs without me here with you? Gail. What were you thinking?" he asked with a massive frown that made him look years older.

"I was very careful. The wolves were right there with me and would have called for you if I'd fallen," she told him. "You can't be with me all the time, Benton. You've got to stop treating me like an invalid. I'm pregnant, not crippled."

White-hot fury burned through her blood like a spewing volcano. Her hormones were acting up again, but this time it was in anger, not tears. Those would probably follow though. They usually did after she'd gotten angry for some reason. Right now, all of her anger was directed at poor Benton. She was tired of being mollycoddled like an old lady. They had to back off some. She knew better than to take chances.

"Now, honey. We're only trying to keep you safe. Now that you're so far along, you don't have the best balance. Your center of gravity has shifted. I promise, we don't think of you as crippled."

"I'm being careful, Benton. I just wanted to make something for the baby with my own hands." Tears brimmed behind her eyes then overflowed like a waterfall.

Benton groaned. "I'm sorry, Gail. I didn't mean to make you cry."

"I can't help it. I got mad, and every time I get angry, I cry." She hiccupped when he wrapped her in his arms.

Gail laid her head against Benton's shoulder until she had better control of her emotions. She pulled back and looked up into his hazel eyes and smiled a watery smile.

"I'm sorry. I really am careful. Next time I'll call for you to go with me."

"Thanks, honey. That would make me feel better," Benton said.

"I need to change out the dehydrator." She turned to get the rest of the meat from the fridge, but Benton stopped her.

"I'll do that while you work on the baby clothes. I'm finished downstairs anyway."

Gail smiled and walked back over to the table to continue working on the baby clothes. She finished stitching up the first one. It looked pretty darn good if she said so herself. She'd show the guys when Travis came back inside. For now, she'd cut out a few more as well as some clothes for diapers. She could stitch them up while she was on the sofa so her feet wouldn't swell as much.

"Have you eaten anything yet, hon?" Benton asked once he'd finished switching out the meat.

"No. I was just thinking that I was a little hungry. I can warm up some stew if you want some." Gail stood and walked over to the fridge.

"I'll warm it up. We can eat in the living room so we don't mess up your sewing," he said.

"I'm finished cutting it all out. I plan to do the sewing part in the living room anyway so that I can put up my feet."

"Good idea." He took the container with the leftover stew from her and poured it into a pan to put over the fire. "Come on and get comfortable. I'll get your sewing kit after I put this on to warm and bring it into the living room for you."

"Thanks." Gail grabbed the pile of cloth she'd cut out and carried it with her.

Sitting down had become an exercise in patience. She had to brace herself on the arm of the couch so that she didn't fall backward when she sat. Gail turned until she could sit with her back to the arm of the chair with a pillow behind her then settled the material over her lap.

Benton finished with the stew and brought her sewing basket to her. Then he repositioned the pillow at her back and settled her feet on another pillow.

"How's that?"

"Perfect."

"Love you, hon."

"I love you, too."

He kissed the top of her head before returning to the fireplace to stir the stew. She watched him for a few seconds, enjoying the play of muscles along his shoulders as he stirred. Both of her men were muscular but not hard. It didn't hurt to lay her head on their chest. It was one of her favorite things to do at night. She'd lay on either Benton or Travis's chest and fall asleep, then sometime in the middle of the night, she'd turn and they'd all spoon until morning.

"What has you smiling with that dreamy look in your eyes?" Benton asked.

"Just thinking how much I love it when you guys hold me. I don't feel quite so bloated next to how big and tall both of you are."

"You're not bloated, and the only place you're big is that basketball that's growing strong inside your belly. Oh," he said with a huge grin. "There's those gorgeous breasts, too. I'm really partial to them."

"Pervert."

"But I'm your pervert, honey."

Gail couldn't help but laugh. They always made her smile.

"Hey, where are you guys?" Travis slammed the back door.

"In here. I'm warming up stew if you're hungry," Benton called out.

Travis walked into the living room and headed straight for Gail. She grinned up at him before he took her mouth in a warm kiss.

"Hey, babe. How are you feeling?"

"I'm great. How goes the tanning?" she asked.

"Slow, but it's coming along. Can't wait to eat though. I was about to pass out from starvation," he told her.

"Look what I made." Gail held up the onesie for the two men to see.

"Hey, that's pretty damn good. When did you make that?" Travis asked.

"This morning. I've cut out a bunch more to sew while I'm being lazy sitting on the couch. I was getting bored just staring at the fire. There's only so many naps a woman can take, you know." Gail shifted her ass in an attempt to settle in a more comfortable position.

"Just as soon as it warms a little more but before we need to get on the planting, we'll drive down to town and raid some stores for baby things," Travis said.

"I can't wait. We need a crib, a baby bed, a playpen, and all the bottles and clothes we can find. We might as well take some of every size since there might not be enough gas to go back later," she said.

"Don't worry, babe. We'll load up on everything. The truck will hold a ton of stuff," he said.

"It wouldn't be a bad idea for you to start a list so that we don't forget something important," Benton suggested.

"I'll do that. I've got plenty of time on my hands to think about it," Gail said.

"Looks like the stew is ready," Benton said. "I'll fill the bowls. Travis, hand the first one to Gail."

Gail's belly chose that moment to grumble, making everyone laugh. Travis handed her the first bowl, and she dug in, suddenly even hungrier now that she had it in front of her. It tasted wonderful even without the flatbread she'd completely forgotten to make. She'd make some after she'd rested for a while.

"Want some more, babe?" Travis asked when she handed him her bowl.

"No thanks. I'm full. I'll probably be hungry again in a couple of hours though."

"That's our baby growing strong. Be sure to feed him every chance you get, babe." Travis rubbed her distended belly before bending down and placing a kiss on it.

"How do you know it will be a he? I think it's going to be a girl," she said.

"I'm hoping for a girl that looks just like you, hon," Benton said.

"I don't care if it's a girl or a boy as long as it's healthy and you don't have a hard labor," Travis said.

"Me, too," she and Benton said at the same time.

Chapter Three

The wolves seemed to pick up on Gail's restlessness as she paced in front of the fire. She couldn't be still as the baby bumped, kicked, and moved inside of her. She wasn't sure what was going on, but figured it was stretching or something. So far it had let her sleep at night, but the night before the little watermelon had moved off and on all night, keeping her awake most of the time.

Everything she'd read in the baby books had said it was normal for there to be periods of movement as the baby developed. She just wasn't expecting it to be so uncomfortable. It didn't hurt so much as irritate her.

Gail wanted to finish up the clothes she'd been making. So far, she had four onesies and six diapers. She'd even managed to make a patchwork quilt that she hoped to find some cloth at the store that wasn't dry rotted for the back of it. She had four more sets of clothes to sew, but she couldn't sit still to work on them.

Wolfie whined as she paced. Gigi and Sasha paced with her while Max lay in front of the fire watching them. Benton was outside working in the shed. Travis was upstairs but would be back down soon. She hoped to be able to rest when he got back or he'd be worried about her. Everything that seemed odd to the men worried them. Maybe he could rub her belly and put the little munchkin to sleep for her.

"Hey, what are you doing up?" Travis asked.

Gail hadn't noticed that he'd walked into the living room. Wolfie whined again.

"What's wrong?" Travis asked with a frown.

"The baby is really active right now. It's uncomfortable to sit. I was thinking maybe you could rub my belly and put her to sleep for me," she told him.

"You bet, babe. Come here." Travis pulled her back in his arms and wrapped them around her to gently rub her belly through her shirt.

"Here, do it like this." Gail lifted her T-shirt and leaned back in his arms.

"Got it." He rubbed both hands over her belly in soothing strokes until the baby slowly settled down.

"Thanks that did it. I'm going to take a nap while she's sleeping," Gail said.

"I'm going to let the wolves out for a bit. I'll be right out the kitchen door if you need me," he said.

She yawned. "Okay. I'm fine."

Gail must have dozed for a while because suddenly, the wolves were back sniffing her before they settled down to rest. She rubbed heads as, one by one, they each curled up and rested their heads on their paws. Having them with her always calmed her. She knew she was safe with them if the men were out of sight.

She wondered what Travis was doing, but wasn't about to call for him. She knew he wouldn't be far. Neither man left her alone for more than a couple of minutes now. Benton hadn't liked that she'd gone upstairs by herself. She was so glad there was a downstairs powder room so that she didn't have to ask one of them to go with her to the bathroom every thirty minutes. At times, the baby seemed to be using her bladder as a pillow so that she had to go constantly.

She shifted on the couch to her side and smiled at Sasha, who had one eye open watching her.

"Go to sleep, Sasha. I'm fine. I'm going to take a nap, too."

The last thing she thought about was that it wouldn't be too long before they went down to town. She had a long list all made up of what they needed.

* * * *

"I found bear tracks way too close to the house, Benton." Travis nodded toward the stream. "There's scratching on several tree trunks indicating that it's claimed this area as its territory."

"Damn. Without a rifle to kill it, the bows aren't going to take one down." Benton shook his head. "What about the larger traps? Do you think they'll work on it?"

"I don't know. The scratches are about five feet off the ground. It could stand anywhere from five feet to six feet tall. They might work. If nothing else, maybe it would scare it off," Travis said.

He was worried that it would wander too close to the house. While Gail was safely inside, there was no telling what a grizzly or even a brown bear would do if it was hungry. They usually ate berries and fish, but were known to attack humans if provoked. Neither he nor Benton were about to provoke a bear, but it still didn't sit well with him.

"I'm going to set the traps out anyway. I'll mark them with the red ribbons around the tree, so you don't accidentally step on one when you're out," he told the other man.

"Be careful. It's going to be tough hunting as long as it's living in the area."

"I wish like hell we still had bullets for the guns." Travis walked toward the shed where the larger traps hung on a nail.

"Do we warn Gail, or keep it from her so she won't worry?" Benton asked.

"Let's not tell her unless the bear moves closer to the house. There's no need to scare her, and you know how she is about the wolves. She'll throw a fit when they go out."

Benton nodded. "Yeah. She'll want to go out with them."

"With the weather warming up, we can plan to go down to town soon. It will do her good to get out and give her something to look forward to."

"How about Saturday? We can get up early, and hopefully get home before it gets dark. We can unload the next day."

Travis winced. "You think it'll take all day?"

"Come on, man. She's a woman, and she's looking for baby things. We'll be lucky to get out of there before dark as it is."

Travis chuckled. "You're right. I'd forgotten how much women like to shop. With no price limit, she'll clear out the stores."

"Get those traps set and hurry back. I need to go back inside to be sure she doesn't do something she has no business doing," Benton said.

"Like make flatbread? She can do things like that, Benton. You're being overprotective. Let her do some things. Sitting around isn't healthy for her either. Remember, the books said the more exercise she got, the easier her labor would be."

"I know, but I worry about her hurting herself. I don't like how her feet swell up when she's on her feet too much."

"So, when they swell, she needs to rest a while. Other than that, let her walk around," Travis said.

"Fine. I'll go easy on her."

Travis threw the traps on the sled and pulled it into the woods behind him. He really wanted to get them out in hopes they could either kill the bear, or make it move its territory somewhere else. If something happened to the wolves, Gail would be devastated. If something happened to Gail, he and Benton would be devastated.

It took him a little over two hours to set the traps where the bear seemed to have traveled. He marked each one with a red ribbon on the tree next to the trap then pulled the empty sled back to the house. After closing it in the shed, he checked the area surrounding the house just to be sure the bear hadn't been that close. Normally they'd avoid humans, but if they smelled food, they wouldn't be shy about trying to find it. He and Benton would need to be extra careful when outside.

He decided they'd feed the wolves inside from then on, so there wouldn't be the scent of food in the air. Luckily, the smoke from the fire would disguise the food they cooked inside the house.

Travis walked inside and removed his boots at the door. He pulled off the jacket and joined Benton and Gail in the living room. Benton was sitting at the far end of the couch rubbing Gail's bare feet.

"Looks like you're doing pretty well," Travis said.

Gail smiled up at him. "Yep. I have my own personal massage therapist. I'd share, but I don't think he'll rub your feet."

"Damn straight I won't. They stink," Benton said.

"Do not. Yours stink," Travis countered.

"That's enough boys. Anyone hungry?" Gail asked.

"Time for her afternoon feeding," Benton teased.

"I can't help it. I'm eating for two. Just a snack." Gail stuck out her bottom lip.

"I'll get it. How about some deer meat between some flatbread?" Travis asked.

"Sounds perfect." Gail stretched out a hand toward him.

Travis held it and squeezed it lightly before padding back into the kitchen to pull out a piece of deer meat they'd taken out of the freezer the night before. He put a nice-sized piece on a cast-iron skillet and carried it back into the living room to set over the fire. It would heat up quickly enough.

"What have you been doing out there?" Gail asked.

"Cleaning the traps, so they'll be ready the next time we need them," he lied.

Travis didn't like lying to Gail, but he didn't want to scare her so that she'd worry anytime they went outside. Plus, she'd fret about the wolves when they went out. It was for the best that she didn't know about the bear.

He turned the meat over in the skillet then, after a few more minutes, carried the skillet back into the kitchen to make her a sandwich. Seeing her bite into it with a smile on her face pleased him. He liked being able to feed her, and knew that Benton really enjoyed it, too. They loved spoiling her, and couldn't wait to have a baby to spoil, as well.

"We've been thinking about going to town soon," Benton said.

"Oh! I can't wait. When?" Gail asked, clapping her hands together.

"How about Saturday, provided the weather is clear?" Travis said.

"Oh, boy. That's perfect. I have my list ready. We should leave really early so we have all day to find everything." Gail's face had transformed into a child's first look at her Christmas toys.

Benton grinned. "That sure made her smile."

"I'm so excited. That's only two days from now. I'm going to rest up, so I'll have plenty of energy to shop," she said.

"If you tire out, they have wheelchairs. One of us will push you around until you've rested up again," Travis told her.

"We should find some cars at one of the other stores to siphon gas from before we even go to shop. I want to be sure we have plenty to get us back," she said.

"That's our job to worry about, hon. All you need to think about is what you want," Benton said.

"Don't worry. I have my list and a head full of stuff that we need for the baby as it grows up," she said. "Oh, and if we have room, we need to look for more canning supplies."

"Got it. I think it's time for a nap for you," Benton said. "Hell. I think I could use a nap, as well."

Travis chuckled as Gail made a face at the other man. Despite her yawn at the mention of taking a nap, she didn't like it when they suggested it. Hell, everything about her tickled him. She was so expressive and fun to be around, when she wasn't in one of her mood swings. Then he either kept out of her way or consoled her if she were crying. Poor Benton couldn't handle it when she cried.

"I'm going upstairs to shower off. I'll join you guys in taking a nap when I finish up," he told them.

"Hurry back down. I missed you while you were outside," Gail told him.

He grinned. "Enough to promise to sleep for an hour or two?" he asked.

"Oh, boo. Yeah. I'm going to take a nap. I guess I am a little tired. I had a good time making flatbread when Benton wasn't fussing at me to hurry up so I could get back on the damn couch again." She stuck her lip out at Benton who'd stood up after finishing her foot massage.

"You'd been on your feet for over an hour. I didn't want them to swell up," he said.

"Children. It's obvious both of you need that nap. I'll be back down soon." Travis left them in the living room and climbed the stairs.

He peeled out of his clothes and hung them up to wear the next day when he went back outside to work. Then he turned on the water to shower. He wished Gail was in there with him. He and Benton loved making her come in the shower. She looked so good sleek from the water. He loved to rub his hands over her slick skin and reach between her legs to rub her clit while Benton sucked on her nipples.

Just the thought of her there with him had his dick hard and needing. He grasped it with a soapy hand and tugged on it. Though they'd made love to her most nights, he could get hard just thinking about her. He always wanted her. Though they had to be more imaginative with her pregnancy, they loved on her as often as they could.

Travis continued pulling on his cock, wrapping his fist around it tighter and tugging faster. He reached between his legs with his other hand to roll and gently squeeze his balls. He was so close, but thinking about burying himself deep inside of Gail's hot, wet cunt finished him off. He came so hard his ass cheeks bunched as he shot his load into his hand and against the shower's tile.

Travis slowly let go of his shaft and leaned with one hand against the back of the shower to catch his breath. His butt muscles ached from the strength of his climax. Fuck but that had felt good. It would feel better to actually be inside of his woman, but that took the edge off for now.

After cleaning up after himself, Travis stepped out of the shower and dried off. He pulled on a pair of sweats then strode toward the stairs. He paused at the top, listening to the voices below. Hearing Benton and Gail chatting warmed his heart. This was his family and he'd do anything to protect them. Even die if it came down to it.

Chapter Four

Gail was up before the sun, super excited that today was the day they were going to town. She eased out of bed, climbing off at the foot, and hurried through her morning rituals and dressed. Then she yelled at the men to get up. Time was a-wasting.

"Come on, guys. It's time to get up. I want to get an early start this morning."

Benton groaned and rolled over. Travis grabbed her pillow and put it over his head.

"What the fuck time is it?" Benton asked.

"Time to get up. The sun is just coming out." Gail walked around the bed to pull the pillow off Travis's head. "Come on. I want to go."

To her surprise, Travis rolled over with a huge smile on his face. "I'm surprised you weren't up earlier."

"Oh, you. Get up and get dressed. I'm going to fix us something to eat while you lazy bones get dressed," she told them.

"Wait until I can walk you downstairs," Benton, ever the worrier, said.

"No. I can walk down by myself. I'll be super careful and hold on to the railing.

"Damn, woman." Benton stood up and scratched his chest. "Can't you wait five minutes?"

"No. I'll see you guys downstairs. I'll have breakfast ready when you get there. Then I'll fix sandwiches to take with us."

"Travis. Do something about her," Benton said as he pulled on his pants.

"Let her go, man. She'll be fine."

Gail grinned and pranced as much as she could, with her rounded belly, out of the room. She was careful negotiating the stairs and held on to the railing like she'd told Benton she'd do. Once she reached the kitchen, Gail got to work preparing a meal of steaks, then while they were warming over the fire, she bagged up some deer jerky and made sandwiches from the warmed meat. By the time the guys had descended the stairs and walked into the kitchen she had everything nearly ready.

"You've been a busy bee," Travis said.

"I can't help being excited. This is going to be so much fun," she said.

"I think while we're looking for what you want, we should look at finding a doggie door to put in the back-porch door so the wolves can go in and out when they need to," Benton said.

"That's a good idea," Travis agreed.

"I don't know. I'd be scared something would come in it." Gail shook her head.

"Well, regardless, with us leaving for the entire day, we're going to have to leave them out or they'll crap all over the house waiting on us to get back," Benton said.

"Leave them out? I'll worry about them while we're gone. What if something happens to them?" she asked.

"They're grown wolves for the most part. They can take care of themselves. Think about it, Gail. They're a pack and not much can hurt a pack of wolves." Benton rubbed up and down her arms.

Gail was afraid to leave them out. Inside she knew that they'd have to, but it hadn't occurred to her until Benton had brought it up. Could she let them stay out without worrying constantly about them?

"I guess you're right. How will we get them not to follow us?" she asked.

"I think they'll stick close to the house. It's their home. You can tell them to stay, and I really think they'll mind you," Travis told her.

"Maybe. I guess there's nothing for it. They'll have to be okay while we're gone. I sure hope I don't worry myself to death about them."

"You'll get into shopping and forget all about it. Don't worry, babe. I hate it when you're upset. It isn't good for you or the baby," Travis said.

Gail sighed. Both men caged her in between them and kissed her on the head, the cheeks, and the back of her neck. That distracted her from her fear for the wolves. She loved it when they hugged her. Of course, Benton had the hardest part since her belly poked between them. Sometimes at night when they first lay down, they'd rub her belly and laugh when the baby kicked at them. Those were happy times for her. She looked forward to it each night.

They'd decided to keep the baby in their room but fix up the one next to them as the nursery for when he or she got much older. They'd put up the baby bed in their room but would be able to move it when they felt comfortable leaving the child alone in the other room. Gail wasn't sure Benton would ever feel comfortable with that.

She smiled. He was so overprotective that it was almost comical. Benton was her worrier, and Travis the one who reasoned with him. Gail loved the diversity between the two men. It made for some fun times when it didn't involve her as much.

I love them both so much. I can't imagine my life without them now. I'm so lucky to have found them.

Well, technically they'd found her. Either way, she was the happiest woman in the world with them. Now that they were going to have a baby, they'd be a real family. She couldn't wait. Well, if she didn't think about the whole hours of labor part.

"I'm going to go warm the truck up. Will you be ready in about five minutes?" Travis asked.

"I'm ready now. The sandwiches and deer jerky are already packed up." She indicated the large cake holder on the counter.

"I'll let the wolves out," Benton said. "When we get ready to leave, you tell them to stay, Gail."

"Okay." She made sure she had her long list of needs in her jacket pocket then sat down to wait for Travis to come get them.

As the wolves walked through the kitchen to go outside, Gail petted each one and ruffled their fur, calling them each by their name. They were so loving toward her. Each one nuzzled her belly before filing outside past Benton. He always gave each one a pet to make sure they saw him as a friend and not a danger to Gail. She knew he worried about them turning on them, but Gail was sure they never would.

"Truck's ready," Travis said as he walked into the living room from the front door. "Let's go, guys."

The men helped her down the porch steps since there wasn't a railing on them. Though the weeds were high outside of the small area the men kept down with a sling blade, it felt like walking through the Serengeti. Travis had told her the wolves loved running through them when they went outside. The wolves whined and gathered around her and Benton.

"Stay. We'll be back tonight. Stay and don't go running off, guys." Gail put as much sternness in her voice as she could.

Mostly they looked to her as their Alpha even though technically Sasha was the Alpha female. She prayed they would stick close to home. She admonished them once more to stay then allowed Travis to walk her around the front of the truck.

"Here you go." Travis helped her into the truck on the passenger side then climbed up behind her.

Benton got into the driver's seat and waited while Travis fastened Gail into her seatbelt. Travis kissed her lightly on the lips then took one of her hands in his. Benton squeezed her thigh as he drove down the drive, the tall weeds waving on either side of them. Though the sun had risen just above the mountains to their left, it was still a little dark as they reached the highway. Benton turned left and they were headed to town.

"I think we should start with everything infant then work our way up to children sizes. Hopefully the clothes aren't dry rotted. Maybe with them hanging they'll be okay." Gail fretted that they wouldn't find much that would work.

"The blue jeans I brought back last time I was there weren't rotted. They were pretty musty-smelling, but a good wash took care of that," Travis said.

Gail must have nodded off at some point because the next thing she knew, they were pulling into a parking lot next to one of the trucks parked near the back. It was a grocery store, so she figured they were going to look for gas for the truck.

She watched as they filled the tank of their truck then filled several gas cans, as well. That would be for the garden tiller. They soon climbed back into the cab with her, and they were off once more.

"Did you fill up the tank?" she asked.

"Yeah. It will be plenty to get us back and for another trip to town if we need to come back for some reason," Travis told her.

Benton drove a few blocks then parked directly in front of the big department store. Benton had her stay in the truck while they made sure there weren't any animals inside. Then they helped her down and all three of them grabbed a cart to shop.

They found the baby section, and Gail loaded up on toys for an infant while Benton and Travis found a baby bed, a playpen, and a stroller. She hadn't thought about the stroller. They left her to load them into the back of the truck as she moved on to bottles and things for feeding as well as baby bibs, diapers, and clothes. She'd filled her basket when the guys returned. Benton exchanged baskets with her and left to add those items to the truck.

"What do you think about the disposable diapers?" Travis asked.

"I don't know if they're any good or not. Let's open one up and check to see if they're okay," she said.

He opened a package and pulled one out. They looked it over and decided it was fine. That led to filling both baskets with all the diapers they could fit in them. Benton finally returned and once again exchanged carts with them.

"I put all the loose items in a plastic bin so they wouldn't get scattered inside the back of the truck," he said.

"Good idea. That's what we need to do with the clothes, as well," Gail said.

For the next three hours they filled plastic bins with cloth diapers, blankets, clothes, and shoes. They worked their way from infant up through teens in both sexes. Travis pointed out that they'd probably end up with several children since there was no such thing as birth control anymore.

"And you know we aren't going to abstain," Travis said with a huge grin that included a sparkle in his light blue eyes.

"Oh, Lord. I hadn't thought about that. You better hope my labor isn't bad or you might not get to touch me for a very long time," Gail warned him.

Benton's mouth quirked down into a frown. She was sure he was thinking about what labor was supposed to be like after reading the pregnancy books they'd been going over.

She smiled. It did them good to think about that.

* * * *

Though it wasn't dark when they finally finished gathering everything on Gail's list, it wasn't far from it. They'd even found more canning supplies and added them to the back of the nearly full truck. Gail was exhausted but so happy. They'd managed to get everything on her list. They made one more stop at the grocery store but locked Gail inside the truck since she was so tired.

"We're going to get all the diapers and any canning supplies they have here while we're in town. There might not be a lot, but every little bit will help," Travis told her.

"If there's any canned goods that haven't popped their tops, we could use some more potatoes," she told them.

"I doubt there will be any. They've probably been raided a long time ago, but we'll look," Benton said.

After they'd gone, Gail leaned against the back of the seat and closed her eyes. She'd had a wonderful time shopping for the baby. As they'd moved up into the older children's clothes she'd thought about the baby growing up over the years. Then she'd thought about having more children and wondered how many children they'd end up with. How would she ever take care of so many, and how would she keep them clothed? Their clothes wouldn't last forever.

By the time the men had returned with baskets full of supplies, she'd just about talked herself into panicking about how they'd take care of so many children. They'd be dressing them in animal skins before long.

"Hey, babe. Why are you looking so upset? Did something happen while we were gone? Why didn't you honk the horn like we told you to do?" Travis climbed up and pulled her into his arms.

"Nothing happened. I was just thinking about how we're going to take care of so many children. Soon there won't be any clothes that are wearable, and we'll have to use animal skins. I guess I worked myself up into a fit worrying about it," Gail told him.

Benton climbed up into the driver's seat. "Is something wrong? Gail, are you feeling bad or hurting? I knew you'd been on your feet too much."

"No, Benton. I'm fine. I was worrying about how we're going to take care of all our children. We're bound to have a lot of them, and I don't know how we're going to feed and dress all of them," she said.

"Aw, honey. Don't think about all of that right now. We'll handle it if that happens. Right now, we only have one baby to take care of. You and the baby," Benton said.

Travis kissed her forehead then slid his arm around her shoulders to pull her as close as the seatbelt would allow.

"Stop worrying and take a little nap. We'll be home before you know it." Travis squeezed her shoulder once more.

Gail tried to relax, but it was a long time before she could relax enough to drift into sleep. Deep in her dreams, she found herself with six kids wearing loincloths and rabbit tops. They were all working in the garden all the way to the little six-year-old who used a small spade to chop up dirt clods. The guys were nowhere in sight, but the wolves were guarding them as they worked under the hot sun.

Then the men returned carrying pails of water for the garden. Over and over they walked from the stream to the garden to empty the water. Gail wondered why they didn't use the hoses they had to water it then realized that they had worn out over the years. How many years had they been living there? She looked at the oldest two children and realized it had been at least thirteen years.

She wiped the sweat from her brow and returned to hoeing out the weeds that seemed to be an ever-present problem. Her children worked right along beside her. Did they even know how to play? She wanted them to have a good childhood, not one where they had to work as hard as she and the guys.

"Hey, babe. Wake up. You're having a dream. Wake up, Gail." Travis was shaking her shoulders with his arm around her.

"Sorry." She yawned.

"What were you dreaming about? You were crying and shaking your head," Benton asked.

"We had six children, but they were all working in the garden with us. You were carrying water from the stream to water the garden, and the children were working instead of playing. I couldn't stand that they didn't have a normal childhood where they ran and played instead of working all the time like us," she explained.

"Don't worry like that, hon. They'll play and have a good life. I promise they will. Yeah, they'll need to help now and then, that's what most kids do. They have chores, but the rest of the time they'll play like children do." Benton patted her leg. "We'll be home in another ten or fifteen minutes."

She couldn't shake the worry that they were overestimating things. How could they possibly grow enough food to feed however many children they had without the kids helping with the garden?

"Don't fret so. I can tell you're still thinking about it," Travis said.

"There's so much stuff to unload," Gail said, then yawned, changing the subject.

"We're going to unload tomorrow. Everything will be fine until then," Travis said.

"That's good. I know you guys are tired and hungry. I'll fix something for supper, then we all need to go to bed early."

"Sounds good to me," Travis said.

"I'll fix supper, honey. You need your feet up. You've been on them way too much today," Benton told her.

"They are a little swollen, but not all that bad. I rode in the wheelchair for a while with Travis pushing me."

Gail giggled, remembering how he'd cut up with her in the chair. He'd zoomed up and down aisles and popped wheelies with her until Benton had fussed. Then they'd shopped with her pointing at what she wanted. After a while, she'd felt like walking again. They'd covered the entire store by the time Travis had declared they needed to head home. She'd gotten everything she'd set out to get and a whole lot more.

"Here we are, babe." Travis unfastened her seatbelt as Benton parked the big truck in the back near the back door.

Immediately the wolves raced up to the truck, jumping and whining until Travis helped Gail down. Then they circled around her, eager to check her out to be sure she was fine. Gail laughed and rubbed all of them. She told each of them how much she'd missed them then allowed Benton to escort her inside with the wolves right behind them.

It was funny to her how Wolfie held the screen door open so that the rest of the wolves could come inside. They were smart animals.

"Go ahead and get on the couch and prop those feet up. I'm going to start on supper," Benton said.

"Where is Travis? What's he doing?" she asked.

"He's putting the cans of gasoline in the shed so everything doesn't smell like gas when we unload it tomorrow. It would have everything closed up in the back of the truck full of fumes." Benton propped her feet up on a pillow then left her to fix their supper.

Gail smiled and relaxed against the pillow behind her back. The dream came back to her in a rush. She tried not to think about it, but the thought that things would get hard as the years went by worried her.

Sasha and Wolfie seemed to pick up on her mood and whined, laying their heads on the edge of the couch to comfort her. She loved them and appreciated that they'd worry with her. She hoped that worry would extend to the children, as well. She'd feel a lot better about them playing outside if the wolves were watching out for them.

She drifted off to thoughts of the wolves playing with the children while keeping watch. It was a good dream this time. One she didn't mind drifting in.

Chapter Five

Gail woke up super excited about the day ahead of them. She turned over to see that both men had already gotten up and were probably even now unloading the truck. She hurried through her morning routine as much as she could with the huge basketball sticking out in front of her. She walked into the kitchen to find the counters full of canning supplies as well as several plastic bins stacked at the back of the little breakfast nook. She started to open one of the bins to see what was in it, but Benton stopped her.

"Don't mess around with those, honey. They're stacked too high. I don't want them to fall over and hurt you." Benton set another one next to the doorway leading into the living room. "Once we have everything unpacked, we're going to carry some of them upstairs into the nursery so that you can go through them a few at a time."

"I'm so excited. I want to get started," Gail said.

He chuckled. "I know."

"Know what?" Travis walked in carrying a bin. He stacked it on top of the one Benton had placed.

"She's too excited to think straight," Benton told him.

"Told you she'd want to dive right in once she woke up." Travis ruffled her hair.

"Have you guys eaten yet?" she asked.

"Yeah, we fixed sandwiches. There's some deer meat warming in a pot next to the fire. Why don't you fix yourself a couple of sandwiches?" Benton suggested.

Gail sighed, but her belly won out. She quickly used the last of the flatbread to make herself something to eat. The meat had been perfectly warm for her. She watched the men carry in bin after bin and stack them in the living room now. She had no idea they'd gathered so much stuff while they'd been in town. She'd be going through them for weeks. It would keep her busy until the baby was born. That thought excited her just as much as shopping had done.

"How am I going to know where to start to find the infant stuff first?" she asked Travis when he stopped to check on her.

"The last things we unload will have the youngest things in them. We'll carry them upstairs first. Then we'll put the rest in the nursery and one of the spare bedrooms," he told her.

"Hadn't thought of that. That's smart," Gail said.

"Hey, we're more than big handsome men. We have brains, too," Travis said.

"I have a brain," Benton said as he carted yet another plastic bin into the room. "You don't."

"Asshole," Travis said.

"Back at you, man."

Gail just shook her head. They were always picking at each other, but it was all in fun. She finished her sandwich and watched them finish unloading the truck. The last things they brought in were the baby bed, changing table, playpen, high chair, and stroller.

"We'll go ahead and put the baby bed together in the bedroom, and the rest can wait until the baby is born," Benton said.

"Make sure to put up the changing table though," she said. "I'll want to put the baby supplies in it. The clothes I'll put in the chest of drawers we emptied out in the nursery," she told them.

"It's too bad we couldn't paint the room for the baby," Travis said. "That dingy white isn't very bright."

"I'll put up the decals and borders we found. That will brighten the room up some," Gail said.

"I'm going to make some more flatbread while you carry things upstairs. I'm down to using the clover flowers and seed pods to make the flour. We're out of the other kind," she told them.

"Remember to put your feet up while it's cooking," Benton reminded her.

"I know, I know. I'll put my feet up. Go work on the baby things." Gail shooed them off then walked into the kitchen.

It took her nearly an hour to make the flour and another hour to pound it into bread once she'd added water and salt. Once she had it like she wanted on the long cookie sheet, she fitted it on the makeshift grate the guys had made to go over the fire when it was banked. She figured it would be ready in an hour or so.

Gail remembered Benton's order and grinned as she sat on the couch and put her feet up. This time she faced the staircase so she could see them when they walked into the room. She could hear them stomping around and the murmur of voices from upstairs. Every once in a while, she heard one of them curse.

Gail figured they were having trouble putting the baby bed together. The playpen would be a piece of cake even for her. When they still hadn't made it downstairs by the time the flatbread was ready, she decided to find out what was going on. She called up the stairs.

"Hey, guys. How's it going up there?"

"Don't climb the stairs, Gail," Benton yelled down. "Everything's fine up here. We just hit a snag with the directions, but we've just about got it all put together now."

"I thought I was hearing you guys cuss. Was that because of the snag you hit?" she asked, unable to stop the huge grin that spread across her face.

"Yeah, Benton thought he could put the rails on without reading the directions. Didn't work out," Travis said.

"That was you, asshole. I told you we needed to go by the directions." Benton's sullen voice made Gail's smile even larger. She loved them.

A lot.

"Let me know when you want something to eat. The flatbread is ready. I'm going to make another batch."

"Did you put your feet up while it was cooking?" Benton appeared at the top of the stairs to look down at her.

"Of course. I put them up, and they're not very swollen at all. I'll put them back up after I make some more flatbread," she told him.

"See that you do. I'm worried that they aren't going all the way down anymore," Benton said.

"I'm getting close to my due time. That's all. They have a lot more weight on them."

"Still, you need to keep off your feet as much as you can." Benton disappeared, so Gail returned to the kitchen to knead up more dough.

* * * *

"See, if you'd followed the damn instructions in the first place, we'd have been finished long before now," Benton fumed.

"I wasn't far off. Just a few steps I skipped is all." Travis sat back on his heels.

Benton wanted to pop the back of the other man's head. He was stubborn like a damn jackass. They'd finally finished the damn baby bed and put together the high chair. Now they were working on the changing table. It was going a little faster than the bed had, thanks to his insistence that they read the directions and follow them.

"Do you think about what we're going to do when Gail goes into labor?" Travis asked him.

"Mostly I try not to think about it," Benton admitted.

"Well, we need to have a plan. She'll panic if we're panicking."

"What do you suggest?"

"Well, the books say that the more she walks when she's in early labor, the better it will be. Gravity will help ease the baby along that way. Then when she's close, one of us will need to help her give birth while the other one holds her hands and let her squeeze them as she pushes.

"I call hand squeezer," Benton immediately said.

"I figured you'd do that. I'll deliver the baby. We need to go ahead and gather what we need in a pan and have it ready. I think the best place will be the kitchen table," Travis said.

"The table? Are you crazy?"

"No. Think about it. We'll pad the table with towels, so it won't be quite so hard, but it will give her something sturdy to hold on to when she needs to push, and we'll be close to the kitchen sink for water."

"I don't know. We need to rethink that," Benton said.

"It will be a lot easier to clean up the mess, too. Think about it, man. We don't have anything big enough to put on the bed to keep from ruining the mattress. The table will be perfect. I can sit in a chair and catch the baby easier than kneeling on a soft bed."

Travis was sure his idea was the best option. Benton would think it over in his own way and agree later. Until then, he'd fuss at Travis about it. That was how Benton did things. Travis was used to him now. They'd been together for so long now it was like arguing with his brother.

"I'll think about it, but that sounds awful hard on Gail to me."

"Not if we pad the table with plenty of towels. We can wash them so it won't matter if they get bloody." Travis nearly burst out laughing at the panicked expression on the other man's face.

"I don't want to talk about it anymore."

"Benton, we need to talk about it before it's too late. I'll gather what we need and have it ready in a dishpan. You bone up on the process in the books as often as you can. We need to have it down good before she actually goes into labor. I don't want Gail to worry about what's happening. She'll have plenty to deal with, with the contractions."

"Fine. I'll read. You deal with the rest."

"You can't pretend it's going to happen, man. You need to have a better attitude about it. We're going to have a son or daughter to love and raise."

"I'm all for that. I can't wait, really, but birthing is what scares me. I'm afraid something bad will happen, and we won't know what to do." Benton's face almost crumpled. "What will we do if something happens to Gail? I couldn't stand it, Travis."

"Neither could I, but we have to be prepared to handle whatever happens and take care of her. Being prepared is the key."

"You're right. I'll bone up on childbirth and gather up all the towels we don't use to have ready. Any idea when she'll most likely go into labor?" Benton asked.

Travis sighed. He didn't have a clue. All any of them knew was that it would be sometime in May or June. They'd have just finished planting and would be keeping the grass out of the garden then.

"What about the wolves?" Benton asked.

"What about them?"

"They can't be around when she goes into labor."

"Why not?"

"All that blood and the baby, man. They might get aggressive."

"I think they'll soothe her. They know she's pregnant. You can tell by how careful they around her and how they nuzzled her belly all the time. They'll know what's going on when she goes into labor. You'll see. I don't think locking them outside will be a good idea. Not only will it upset Gail, which we sure as hell don't want to do while she's in labor, but they'll go wild outside trying to get inside to check on her."

"Fuck. I don't like them being around her. I sure as hell don't trust them."

"They're good to have around. I think the fact that they're here is what has kept that damn bear out of the house area," Travis said.

"Maybe so." Benton didn't sound convinced.

"Stop worrying now. We need to get this damn stroller finished and get down to our woman."

Travis worked next to Benton for the next thirty minutes then stood and grinned at the stroller. They'd done it. Everything was together. He checked out the baby bed one more time before helping Benton clean up the boxes, paper, and tools. They carried everything back down and outside to burn later.

"Everything go together okay?" Gail asked when they'd returned to the living room.

"All put together. It only took us all afternoon," Benton complained.

"We had a lot to work on," Travis said.

"I took out some steaks. Feel like cooking them when they are thawed enough?" she asked.

"No problem," Travis told her. "Are you feeling bad?"

"No, I just want to rest up some, so I can go through the bins you carry upstairs for me. I want to put away some of it before time for bed."

"Don't overdo it, hon. You've already made two batches of bread today." Benton shot a look at Travis.

Travis knew Benton wanted him to back him up on that. Instead he compromised.

"We'll see how you feel after supper. If you're not too worn out or your feet too swollen, we'll carry up one bin for you to go through."

"You're getting as bad as Benton with ordering me around. If I tell you to carry that thing upstairs, you're going to do it or suffer my wrath," Gail told him with a huff.

Travis knew he would regret it, but she was so darn cute he couldn't help but burst out laughing. Her face grew a rosy shade of pink as she propped her hands on her waist with her baby belly sticking out. She aimed him a look meant to slay.

"Don't you dare laugh at me, Trenton Lawrence. You'll do without for the remainder of my pregnancy and ten weeks after to boot," she said.

"Six weeks," Trenton teased.

"Ten weeks if you and Benton don't behave yourselves."

"Travis, shut the fuck up." Benton pulled Gail into his arms.

"Shutting the fuck up."

Chapter Six

"Please, Travis, Benton? I want you both. I'm so fucking horny I'm going to combust if you don't play with me. Please." Gail wanted to knock both men over the head.

They didn't want to hurt her by fucking her. She was tired of them fingering her and licking her pussy. God, she'd never thought she'd say that to them. It seemed like a sin to even think about it, but she was horny and only their big hard cocks would do.

"We aren't both taking you while you're pregnant. It's too much with the baby there, too. Once you've recovered we'll be all for it," Benton said.

"Travis, you're usually the voice of reason. Tell Benton it's okay," she said.

"I'm with Benton on this," Travis told her.

"The books said having sex all the way up until I go into labor is safe and fine. Why are you being this way?"

"The books were talking about normal, one-on-one sex, babe. Not a two-for-one. Benton can take care of you, and I'll come in that potty mouth of yours. Remember that when the baby comes you can't talk like that," he said, mimicking her telling them repeatedly not to curse in front of the baby.

"Damn you guys. I need you," she whined.

Ever since she'd gotten pregnant, she'd had an overactive libido, wanting sex all the time. The guys had thoroughly enjoyed it until she'd gotten so far along that her baby belly reminded them that she was carrying their child. Then they'd backed off some, and lately they'd refused to take her at the same time.

"Fine. One at a time, but I want both of you. I miss having you inside of me every night," she pouted.

"You can stick that lip back in where it's supposed to be. You're at least eight months pregnant, babe. We aren't taking any chances that we'll cause you to go into labor early. Nice and easy, or not at all," Travis said, crossing his arms.

Gail sighed. "Okay."

Benton smiled and climbed onto the bed, laying on his back. They'd figured out that either doggy style or cowgirl were the only comfortable ways they could screw now. Gail crawled over to take his hard cock inside of her. Her pussy was already wet and ready for him. She got wet all the time now. It was like when it got time for bed, she soaked her panties.

The instant she lowered herself onto Benton's hard shaft, Gail felt good. She moaned then lifted and dropped back down. Benton helped her since she was ripe with their baby. She rode him as he pumped his hips up into her.

"Oh, God, Benton. You feel so good inside of me," Gail said.

"Your pussy is hot and wet, hon. Feels so fucking good." Benton was watching where their bodies were joined.

Gail loved how excited he got when he watched her take his hard dick deep inside her body. It was a turn-on for her to see the slack expression on his face the closer he came to climax. She wasn't far behind. Her body was tightening, primed and ready to come. All it would take was a good swipe across her clit. She almost reached down to do it herself, but knew that Benton enjoyed doing that for her. She groaned as he pulled back then let her sink back down on him while he thrust upward once more.

"Your pussy feels so damn good, Gail. I love sinking my cock all the way in that tight cunt." Benton's words had her even closer.

"Please, Benton. I need to come. I'm so close."

"I've got you. I'll take care of you. Just a few seconds longer. You feel too good to stop."

Gail knew he'd go over with her when she squeezed down on him during her orgasm. He always did. Hers always triggered both men's. It was amazing how they nearly always came together.

"There we go, hon. Come for me." Benton rubbed the pad of his callused thumb over her clit, and just like that, she shot over.

Her strangled scream covered Benton's shout as he shot cum deep inside of her. She shivered over him as he thrust a few more times before collapsing back against the mattress once more.

Gail couldn't fall over on top of him, as she'd use to do, with her belly so large. Now, she allowed Travis to help her off Benton's softening cock to curl up next to him. She'd take care of Travis once she'd caught her breath. There was no way she'd leave him lacking. He was always so patient with her when it came to sex.

"That was so fucking good, hon. Are you okay?" he asked.

"Mmm. Great. Let me bask," she teased.

"Bask? What does that mean?" Benton asked.

"It means enjoy the afterglow, taking in the moment." Gail smiled up at him.

"So, it was good for you, huh?" he asked.

"Always. It's always good with both of you guys."

She rolled over and grasped Travis's cock before he could move away. He groaned as she squeezed it.

"Rest a while, babe. I can wait. You'll wear yourself out." Travis tugged gently on her hair.

"I'm all rested and want to suck your dick now. Get off the bed, Travis."

Gail scooted over to sit on the edge so that Travis would be in the perfect position for her to take him in her mouth. Instead of following her directions, he sat next to her.

"You know you don't have to do this, babe. I'm fine. I can wait until next time. Both of us don't have to come every time. We won't think any less of you or be jealous of the other one," he said.

Travis wrapped his arm around her shoulders and tugged on her hair again. He was always playing with her hair. She knew he loved it when she let it drag across his chest or his cock.

"I know, Travis, but I wouldn't do it if I didn't want to or feel like it. I want to suck you. I want to feel that thick part of you in my mouth where I can lick and suck and tease you with my tongue."

Travis groaned like she knew he would. She could talk either one of them into an erection every time. She loved that about them. They wanted her at the drop of a word or phrase.

"If you're sure." Travis looked at her before standing up, having seen what he needed to see in her eyes.

Gail grasped his shaft and pumped it once to give her that little pearl of pre-cum she loved to taste. She licked over the slit and moaned at the salty taste of him. Then she licked up the underside of his dick before sucking him deep inside her mouth. She reached around and squeezed his ass cheeks before using one hand to massage his balls and the other hand to grasp his cock. While she held the stiff shaft in her mouth, Gail sucked him in then came back off of him as she swirled the tip of her tongue around the underside of the crown of his dick.

"Fuck, your mouth is so damn hot and wet." Travis tangled both hands in her hair.

He didn't try to hold her head or force her down on him. He just held her hair in his hands, occasionally tugging on it in the throes of his excitement. Gail licked then sucked him back down before swallowing around him.

"God, yes. Just like that. Holy hell, babe. That's so good."

Gail moaned around his cock then used just a little of her teeth to rake over his shaft before going all the way back down on him and swallowing again.

She felt him when he went up on his toes as she swallowed. He was close. Just on the edge. She could always tell by that. Gail moved up and down his shaft in quick little sucks then raked her nails over his balls while she swallowed around his cock at the same time. He dug his nails into her scalp and shouted as he emptied his seed down her throat. Gail had to swallow fast as he filled her mouth, as well. He pulled back when she kept sucking.

"Fuck, babe. That was amazing. You're so damn good at sucking me off. I have a hard time deciding which I want more, your pussy, your ass, or your mouth," he said.

"Well, since I love anywhere you take me, that's fine. I like that you want me, Travis." She turned to Benton. "I love it that both of you get hard for me all the time. It makes me feel sexy even though I'm fat as a pig."

"You're not fat at all," Benton said. "You're full of baby. There's not an ounce of fat on you. I'd hoped you'd gain a little more weight with the pregnancy, but you're all baby."

"If you say so." Gail sighed and stood. "I need to clean up. I'll be right back."

She returned a few minutes later to find Benton snoring while Travis sat on the other side of the bed waiting on her. She chuckled softly, pointing at the other man.

"Yeah, you wore him out. I don't think you were gone more than a few seconds before he was sawing logs." Travis helped her climb up on the bed then curled around her with one hand on her belly. "Good night, babe."

"Night, Travis."

* * * *

Several days later, Gail rubbed her lower back. Lately it had started to ache when she was on her feet for very long at a time. She'd just finished making two pans of flatbread and had three steaks covered with a cloth defrosting next to the fire. Travis had gone hunting for some fresh meat for a change, and Benton was dozing in his chair. She walked across to the table and set down to rest her back.

Sasha and Wolfie laid their heads in her lap. She rubbed them absently when Benton walked in.

"You look tired, honey. You need to rest some," he said.

"I'm not really tired. My back aches. That's all. I guess having this huge baby belly sticking out is pulling on it."

"That's why you need to go lay down for a while. When Travis gets back, I'll cook the steaks while he takes care of whatever he kills."

"I hope it's not deer. I'm ready for a nice rabbit or a few squirrels."

"I agree. Never thought I'd get tired of deer," Benton said.

He urged her into the living room where he sat down at the opposite end of the couch to rub her feet while she lay down.

"Will you rub my back instead?" she asked.

"Of course. Turn over so I can get to it."

Gail faced the back of the couch and moaned the instant Benton began massaging her lower back.

"That feels better than sex."

"I sure as hell hope not," Benton teased.

"Close enough."

"You don't think you're in labor, do you?" Benton asked a few seconds later.

"No. It's not back labor. I think that usually hits your back and runs around to your belly. I'm not quite due yet. It's just back pain from the pull of my belly on my back. I'm fine. Especially with your hands kneading my back muscles."

"I live to serve, hon. Is the pain going away now?"

"It's much better. I don't think it's going to go completely away until I have this bowling ball," she said.

"I hate that you're so uncomfortable." Benton stood and leaned over to kiss her gently on the lips. "I'll rub your back until you fall asleep. Sound good?"

"Mmm, sounds perfect."

Minutes later, she was still awake, but feeling much better. She wasn't really sleepy and felt fairly good despite her back aching.

"I need to get up, Benton. I need to pee."

"I thought you were going to take a nap." He helped her roll over so that she didn't roll off the couch.

"I'm not sleepy. Now my back feels better, so I want to go work on the nursery some."

"I'll help you up the stairs after you go to the bathroom. I'll wait right outside the door."

"Benton. I'm not an invalid. I can manage to pee by myself. At least sit on the couch until I'm ready. I don't want you listening outside the damn door."

"Sorry." Benton winced at her sharp voice.

Gail sighed. She couldn't seem to keep her hormones from pushing her from one extreme to the other. The poor men got the brunt of it.

As soon as she'd finished in the bathroom, Benton was back, ushering her up the stairs with him behind her in case she lost her footing or became overbalanced. It was so sweet that he was that careful with her, but sometimes he smothered her with it.

Once she'd negotiated the stairs without giving Benton a heart attack, she walked into the room they'd designated as the nursery and sat in the chair they'd placed up there for her.

"Still feeling okay?" Benton asked.

"I'm fine. Well, except for the kicking. I swear this is a soccer player rolling around in my belly." Gail grabbed Benton's hand and placed over the spot where the baby was bumping against her belly.

"Wow, he is a little kicker. As much as I like that he's moving around so much, I wish he'd give you some rest." Benton lifted his hand to cup her face. "You haven't been sleeping well these last few weeks."

"It's all part of being pregnant. I'll be fine. Once the baby arrives, I'll get more sleep with both you and Travis there to help take care of him."

"We'll take care of him so you can rest. There's three of us to take turns. You can rest in between feedings."

Benton kissed the top of her nose then turned to leave. He stopped and turned to smile over his shoulder.

"Remember to call down if you need anything. I'll be in the living room getting the steaks ready."

She nodded then waved him off. Gail opened one of the plastic bins and started going through the cute baby clothes. She'd already put away the supplies like baby powder and baby lotion. She'd had the guys put all the larger-size disposable diapers in the closet in there and in one of the other bedrooms.

Now she sifted through the infant and baby clothes to put them away in the chest of drawers. She enjoyed playing with them as she held each one up before folding it and setting it in the drawer. There were so many. She'd never have to worry about running out for this baby and maybe one more. After that, they'd get threadbare.

Once again, she worried about what they'd do for supplies if they kept having children. With no birth control she could conceivably have upwards of eight or so babies. That worried her. Not only because they'd have to enlarge the garden to feed all of them, but also because they wouldn't have enough room for them or clothes to fit all of them by that time.

Gail struggled to banish the worry. They couldn't worry about the future right then. She had one baby to worry about, and that's all she needed to think about for now. She'd breastfeed the baby as long as she could, which would keep her from getting pregnant according to the baby books. At least for five or six months.

"How are you doing?" Benton asked as she held up yet another cute outfit.

"Great. These are all so cute. What are you doing? Checking up on me again?"

"I just wanted to be sure you didn't need anything. I'm about to cook the steaks. Travis will be home soon."

"I'm fine, Benton. Go cook. Tell Travis to come get me when he gets back. I'm already hungry," she said.

"Call if you need anything, or if you want to come downstairs. It's too dangerous for you to go down them by yourself."

"I know, I know. I'll call." Gail waved him away and pulled out a pair of socks that looked entirely too small to fit anyone, even an infant.

Benton walked out of the room. She heard his heavy tread down the stairs, then the room grew silent. Gail finished unloading the bin and covered it with the lid before standing and pushing it across the floor next to the other empty bins. The men planned to store them in the cellar.

Sasha and Max were upstairs with her. They followed her out of the nursery into the master bedroom. They weren't allowed in there at night, but followed her like faithful companions as she laid a folded baby blanket at the foot of the baby bed. Inside were two that she'd made as well as a rabbit fur just to lay over the baby's feet for warmth. They'd decided that the fur might not be safe too close to the baby's face.

"What do you think, Sasha? Are we ready for the baby now?"

"If Sasha answers you, I'm hightailing it out of here." Travis smiled when she turned and hurried across the floor to wrap her arms around him.

"You're back! What did you get?" she asked.

"Two rabbits. We'll have it for lunch and supper tomorrow. Benton has the steaks done if you're ready to go down now," he said.

"I'm starving. Let's go."

Gail looked back at the baby bed one last time then allowed Travis to lead her toward the stairs with the wolves following behind them.

Chapter Seven

May rolled in with comfortable temperatures and growing plants in the garden. They'd managed to get the seeds planted before the April showers had begun. Both men worried they'd planted too soon, but there'd been no more freezing nights to worry about. Now the plants, along with some stubborn weeds, were growing strong and tall. The men spent most of each day working among the plants in an effort to keep the weeds down.

Gail tried to help, but they flat refused to allow her to step foot off the back porch. She spent the mornings doing some light cleaning while they worked outside. Then she sat on the back porch watching them and mending their clothes. She'd found an old-fashioned round lightbulb to use to fill out the toes of the socks so she could mend them. The holes in the men's jeans took making patches, but she managed just fine.

"How are you doing, babe?" Travis asked when he'd reached the door of the porch.

"I'm good. Just doing some sewing. How are y'all doing out there? Ready for something to drink?" she asked.

"That would be great. I'll wait here to take Benton's out to him."

"Come on inside and sit down. You're bound to be tired."

"Too dirty to track dirt in. We'll need to take our boots off out here. There's still some muddy places in the lower part of the garden."

"I'll have your drinks ready in a jiffy."

Gail waddled into the kitchen and got down two plastic cups for them to take outside. She poured the cold tea into the cups then carried them out to Travis.

"Thanks, babe. Go on inside and rest. It's too warm out here for you."

"It feels better out here than in the house. I have the windows up to let in some fresh air. I'm fine, Travis. Go give Benton his tea. If I get tired, I'll go lie down on the couch for a little while."

"Holding you to it, Gail."

While she maneuvered her way back onto the chair, Travis carried the other cup over to where Benton was whacking at a stubborn stalk of some sort of weed. It was probably a dandelion, but they didn't need them in their garden. There were plenty of them around to dry later for the tea.

Gail smiled at the pair of them. Her men were strong, hardworking, and loving toward her. They had never gotten angry with her, only upset or worried when they thought she wasn't taking care of herself. She looked down at her rounded belly that had taught her the meaning of waddle like a duck and reaching for things she could no longer grab with her swollen baby bump.

It's not a bump anymore. It's more like a bowling ball or a watermelon. I can't believe I'm going to have a baby soon.

She couldn't help but worry a little about what kind of mother she'd be, but the guys always put her mind at ease when she worried out loud. They promised she'd be wonderful. They'd reminded her of how well she'd taken care of the wolf pups and how great they'd turned out. She reached down and petted Gigi. The female wolf had become her constant companion if any of the other wolves were outside with the men.

She was tired, and her back had been hurting almost nonstop for the last few days. She levered herself to the edge of the chair and slowly pushed up before standing for a few seconds to be sure she had her balance. That was another thing about being pregnant she hadn't expected. Her center of gravity had changed.

I wish my back would stop hurting. I can't get comfortable with it aching like it is.

Gail wobbled inside then poured herself a glass of tea. She carried it into the living room where she lowered herself to the couch and swung her legs up so she could rest on the pillow against the arm of the couch. The tea went down good, but she didn't drink much since it would mean she'd have to go to the bathroom before she'd even relaxed.

Gigi followed her in and circled twice before stretching out on the floor near her head. She seemed to know better than to get close to where Gail's feet would need to be when she got up.

"You're such a good girl, Gigi. You and the others watch out for all of us. I can't believe how much you've grown. I guess you're pretty much full grown now."

Gail closed her eyes and tried to rest. The aching in her back circled around to her belly, making her arch her back in protest. That one had hurt.

She tried to turn to one side and take the pressure off her aching muscles, but nothing seemed to help. She'd just get settled when ten or fifteen minutes later the terrible cramping to her back then her stomach grabbed her once more.

After nearly thirty minutes of tossing around as much as she could with her heavy body, Gail sat up and groaned. Gigi stood and rubbed her nose against Gail's belly, seeming to try to ease her discomfort. When Gail felt the pain grab at her again, Gigi whined and nudged her belly.

"What is it, girl? What's got you so upset?"

Then it hit her. Gail felt herself go numb with fear. She was in labor. Was it too soon? She had no way of knowing since she wasn't completely sure of her due date. May or June was as close as she'd been able to figure out. She needed to get the guys.

No. I'll wait until the contractions are a little closer together. First babies always take longer to birth. There's no reason to upset them until I'm closer to having the baby. I sure hope my labor isn't nearly as long as they caution it can be in the baby books. The guys will have their own babies if it is.

Gail smiled. The thought of them going through the labor she would be going through amused her. Then another pain hit, and all she could think about was breathing and moving any way that would help it fade away. Once it was gone, she shoved her way up and headed for the bathroom. The baby was once again sitting on her bladder.

Two hours later Gail had had enough. She needed her men there to help her. While Gigi had been wonderful walking the floor with her, she wanted them by her side. The wolf whined and nudged her whenever she stopped to sit for a while as if telling her she needed to get someone to help her.

"Don't worry, girl. I'm ready for them now. I better stand back from the door when I call them, or they'll knock me down trying to get inside." She chuckled at the thought.

The short shuffle to the back door seemed to take forever. She stopped by the kitchen table to grasp one of the chair backs when a pain hit again, twisting at her stomach like a giant hand gripping her there. She panted through it, though it didn't seem to help much as she stood there. Then she drew in a calming deep breath and let it out slowly before waddling out of the kitchen to open the screen door of the porch.

"Travis! Benton! Can you come here?" she called out.

Gail couldn't see them, so they had to be at the very back of the garden where the corn was growing or inside the shed for some reason. She called out again before Benton came running from the far back of the yard.

"What's wrong? Are you okay?" he yelled as he neared the back porch. All three of the other wolves followed in his wake.

"I'm okay, but I think I'm in labor."

"You're in labor? Why aren't you lying down? Go on. I'm right behind you, honey."

Benton called out for Travis then followed Gail into the house with a soothing hand against her lower back.

"Come on now. Let's get you comfortable in one of the recliners. You'll feel better with your legs up and the support of the chair back. The arm of the couch can't be very comfortable," he said.

"What's wrong with Gail?" Travis skidded to a stop when he saw Gail in the recliner.

"She thinks she's in labor. We need to stick close to her now," Benton said.

"I'll go put up all the tools then be right back." He walked over to where Gail lay back and kissed her cheek. "I'll be right back, babe."

"I'm fine. You know this is probably going to take a while. There's no hurry so be careful," she told him.

Travis nodded then ran out of the room. She heard the back door slam behind him then the louder bang of the screen door on the porch. She sighed. She'd known they would go crazy once she told them.

"How long have you been having contractions, honey?" Benton asked.

"About an hour or so. I think I've been in labor all day, though. My back's been aching in cycles, but it just started about an hour ago circling around to my stomach."

"Why didn't call for us sooner? You shouldn't have had to go through that alone."

"You can't do anything, and we both know from the baby books that this is going to take a while. I just wish I'd been around one of the other women who were pregnant when they had their babies so I'd know what to expect. This is kind of scary, Benton."

He cupped her cheek in his hand. "Don't worry. We're going to be right here and help you through it. We might not have gone through one of those classes the books talked about, but we know what we're supposed to do to help you."

A pain gripped Gail so that she grasped the arms of the chair as she tried to breathe through it. Benton rubbed her belly and murmured in her ear to pant as he tried to soothe her. Once it had passed, Gail closed her eyes and tried to relax. Benton continued to rub light circles around her abdomen.

After what seemed like an hour, Travis returned with a warm, wet cloth. He wiped her face and neck then kissed her before tossing the wet cloth over the arm of the other recliner.

"How's she doing?" he asked Benton.

"Pains are about every twenty minutes right now. Next time one comes, reach behind her and rub her lower back while I rub her belly. We'll switch places each time," Benton told him.

Gail smiled at their sharing of duties in an effort to help her through the labor. With the way it had moved from her back to her belly, she was sure now that this was it. Sometime, in the not so distant future, she hoped, she was going to have a baby to love and care for.

She opened her eyes when the next pain tightened her back and belly. The wolves were circling the chair with Sasha leaning against the foot part of the recliner with her head resting next to Gail's swollen ankles. She couldn't help but smile through the pain at the fact that the wolves were right there with her, just like her men.

"Easy, babe. Try to pant like we practiced with the book. Blow out the air to help relax those muscles. There we go." Travis soothed her with his voice as he rubbed her lower back.

Hours seemed to pass when she felt the need to go to the bathroom once more. The men helped her up, steadying her when she first stood. They walked her there then paced with her while she walked through the next pain.

"You need to get back in the recliner, honey. I don't want you to fall while you're having a pain like that." Benton's hovering hands spoke to his nervousness.

"I need to walk some. Remember, the book said walking would help progress the labor and make it less stressful." Gail knew her voice sharpened with him, but couldn't help it.

The pains were every ten minutes now. They'd remained at twelve for a long time, but now that they were ten, she knew she needed to move around for a while. It would help the baby to move into position and help her cervix to dilate. The sooner the better. Much more of the gripping pain and Gail was sure she was going to hurt someone.

"Walk slow, babe. We don't want you to fall. Just take it easy."

Gail bit her tongue before she told him to take it easy with an explicative at the end. They were just trying to help her, and they were just as nervous about all of it as she was, but their hovering was making her crazy. She felt like slapping both of them over the head in frustration. The assholes. They were the reason she was in this mess.

"I can feel it starting again," Benton said as he held one hand against her low back.

"Pant, babe. I've got you." Travis rubbed light circles around her distended belly, pushing out his breath in an attempt to encourage her.

He was doing a pretty crappy job of helping the way he breathed in and out with pursed lips.

"You're not doing it right," Benton said as she panted through the pain.

"Don't fucking tell me I'm not doing it right. I'm the one needing to do it," she yelled.

"Easy, babe. Just purse your lips and push the air out. Breathe in then push it out." Travis rubbed her arms even though she narrowed her eyes at him.

Gail tried to calm down so that she didn't say something she'd regret. A little cursing was to be expected, but she honestly didn't want to be mean to them. Still, when the next pain grabbed her, she was hard-pressed to keep her mouth shut when they rubbed and whispered how good she was doing.

"Time to sit down for a little while, babe. You're wearing yourself out. Just for a little while to get your feet up." Travis steered her toward the recliner and helped her to sit while Benton manned the handle to raise her legs.

Gail moaned when her back sank into the now soft cushion. Not much later, the soft cushion became a concrete board to her tight back as another contraction tightened every muscle in the middle of her body. She felt as if her belly would burst open at any minute. She couldn't stop the tears that slid down her face until it passed. Both men were solid rocks as they helped her through the pain, but once it was over they wrung their hands and tried to figure out how to make the next one easier on her.

"Stop worrying. It's going to hurt. That's all there is to it. Just don't expect there to be another baby in the future. This sucks," she told them.

Nearly an hour later Gail demanded to get back up and walk. She needed to go to the bathroom again anyway. The pressure on her bladder had increased to the point she was afraid she'd lose control of it if she didn't hurry.

"Careful, honey. Let us help you," Benton cooed.

"I can go to the freaking bathroom in my sleep. I don't need your help."

She could hear them murmuring through the door as she stood in front of the sink and washed her face. They were worried, she knew, but she couldn't help but snap at them when the pains got too hard. They'd forgive her once the baby came. She'd forgive them, as well.

Might be a few days or even weeks before I forget how this feels though.

She finally opened the door and let them take her arms to lead her back and forth across the living room floor. She'd made about five trips when water gushed from between her legs. Both men panicked as she sighed. Her water had finally broken.

Chapter Eight

Benton looked down at the water on the floor then back up at his woman. Fear conquered the urge to pull her into his arms. He didn't want to squeeze anything else out of her, but he desperately wanted to hold her.

"The baby's coming!" Travis yelled. "We need to get her to the table. I need to get the towels and the pan."

"Wait, guys," Gail called out in a weak voice.

"You go get everything ready," Benton began. "I'll hold her until you're ready."

Travis ran off toward the kitchen then returned to race upstairs as if he couldn't figure out where he was supposed to go. Gail shook her head and looked up at Benton. He smiled down at her but figured the smile wasn't all it should have been.

"You're going to be just fine, hon. We're getting everything ready for the baby now. We've talked about it and figured out what needs to be done. You'll see. We've got everything planned."

"Don't you think you should have talked to me about it? I can't believe we didn't all sit down and plan this." Gail's voice had begun to get shrill.

Benton tried to calm her down by rubbing her back for her. She didn't seem to notice. Instead she paced faster with him, stumbling in an effort to keep up while making sure she didn't fall. The wolves stayed out from under their feet, but they were pacing right beside her. The damn things knew what was going on. He was sure of it.

"Got the padding," Travis said as he raced past them once more.

"He's going to kill himself if he doesn't slow down," Gail muttered.

"Travis is just as excited as I am, but we're worried about you. Usually the baby is close when your water breaks. At least the books say so. Do you feel any pressure like you need to push?" Benton asked her.

She turned narrowed eyes at him. "The only thing I want to push right now is you. Down those damn stairs."

Benton winced. Yep, she had to be getting close. She was getting to the dangerous phase for men. The part where she cursed them and threatened bodily harm. They needed to get her on the table and in position soon.

"What in the hell is Travis doing to the kitchen table?" Gail demanded.

"He's getting it ready for you, hon. We wanted to pad it for you so it wouldn't be too hard on your back."

"Why can't I get in the bed?" she demanded.

"The books say that having a baby in bed can be hard without something firm underneath you." Benton nearly took a step back at the look on her face.

"I'm not climbing up on the fucking table that we eat on. No way, no how," she yelled at him.

"But, honey…"

"Don't 'honey' me. Take me upstairs. Get some of that plastic sheeting we got from the store and put it on the foot of the bed." She shook her head. "I can't believe you planned to make me give birth on the freaking kitchen table. What if you let the baby slip out of your hands? He would have hit the hard kitchen floor. That is *not* happening."

Benton panicked. She was getting more and more angry by the second. He called for Travis.

"Change of plans. Go out to the shed and get that roll of plastic sheeting. Carry it upstairs and tear off a piece to put over the foot of the bed and the floor. Then carry everything from down here to up there."

"What about the table?" he asked.

"Don't ever say that again," Gail yelled.

Travis jerked his eyes from her to Benton. He shook his head at the other man. Travis needed to get on board with the new plans before Gail hit him over the head with something.

"Ow. Oh, oh. Damn this hurts." She grabbed both of Benton's hands, and squeezed them hard enough he winced, trying not to make a sound.

"Try to breathe through it, hon. With me." He tried to show her the panting he'd been practicing ever since he'd read over the baby book for the fifth time.

The book, fuck.

They needed to carry the book upstairs with them. He'd tell Travis to get it once he'd finished carrying everything to their bedroom. Until then, he walked with Gail until she was too tired to walk but didn't want to sit on the recliner. He grabbed a blanket off the back of the couch and draped it over the sofa cushion so she could sit without staining the material. They'd clean up the floor later.

"I got the plastic and the basin. I'll come back down for the towels next," Travis called out as he raced past them.

Benton rubbed Gail's low back then her belly as Travis raced back and forth until he had everything situated upstairs. At least Benton hoped he had it set up right. For all he knew, the other man had just dropped everything on the floor and hadn't even covered the bed with the plastic. Travis was just as nervous and worried as he. He had to relax so that Gail would. They both needed to.

He looked over at the wolves and how they were sitting around, but weren't pacing as if they were just as worried. Though he'd been against keeping them then once they'd grown and proved themselves to be protective of Gail, he'd been reluctant but accepting, Benton couldn't help but approve of the way they'd stood by her and kept her company when he and Travis were out working. He had to admit that it had kept him from worrying nearly as much as he would have otherwise.

Now, as he and Travis helped Gail off the couch, they stood, as well, ready for whatever they were going to do next. He wasn't sure about having them in the bedroom during the birthing. He was afraid the blood would arouse some sort of feral instinct in them to attack.

They helped Gail upstairs, having to pause midway while she fought through yet another contraction. They were coming every six to seven minutes now. It was time to get her on that bed.

"How are you doing?" Travis asked as they reached the landing.

"I'm hurting. How do you think I'm doing?" she bit out at the other man.

"I'm sorry, babe. I'm so sorry you're hurting."

"I know. I know. I can't help but yell at you guys. This hurts more than I thought it would, and this isn't even the worst of it." Gail huffed out a breath before they walked with her into the master bedroom.

To Benton's relief, Travis had more than handled getting everything ready. Plastic sheeting covered the bed with several towels underneath and one towel on top of the plastic to make it more comfortable for Gail. The plastic extended down for about four feet across the floor where the edges all had towels to absorb anything that spilled over. There were towels where whichever of them finally decided to kneel there to catch the baby to help their knees.

Sitting at the foot of the bed to one side was the little baby bed already decked out with towels so they could clean the baby up. The baby book was farther up on the bed where the other of them would be kneeling to coach Gail through the labor. He wasn't sure who would do what now. He wasn't sure what would be the more stressful position.

"Here you go, babe. Let's get you comfortable." Travis held out his hand to Gail.

Benton helped her climb up on the bed and roll over until she was in the center of the plastic sheet with her legs hanging off the bed. He unfastened her pants and, with Travis's help, slid them down her body to pull them off once they had her shoes off, as well. Then Travis pulled her shirt off and draped a soft blanket over her chest. The book had mentioned that the mother wouldn't want many clothes on because she'd get hot and sweaty and would feel restricted.

"Let's scoot you back some for now," Benton told her.

Travis got behind her and pulled as Benton helped him slide her farther back on the bed so that her legs weren't hanging off it. Then he looked at the other man and realized he'd been designated as the doctor as far as positions went.

Fuck.

"Gail, bend your legs and spread them apart so I can check to see if the baby is crowning or not."

"What? Crowning?"

"If the baby's head is showing or not, hon. Bend your legs and let's see where you are."

"Do you have any idea of what you're looking for?" she demanded after spreading her legs.

"Travis and I've both studied the book several times, honey. You're going to be fine."

He bent over and spread her slightly but didn't see anything. He knew that he should use his fingers to check her cervix, but wasn't sure he'd know what he was feeling. He decided that the best thing to do was to wait until she had another contraction then see if he could tell anything with her bearing down.

"I'm going to wash my hands. I'll be right back. Then I'll check to see if you're dilated any," he said.

Travis nodded at him as he held one of Gail's hands in his. The other man would do his best to help her through the labor. Benton just prayed there were no complications since he didn't know the first thing about what to do if something outside of the book happened.

Once he'd scrubbed his hands, Benton returned to kneel between her legs and lean in toward her spread legs. As many times as he'd been down there, this was so different. He almost felt like a voyeur, someone who shouldn't be staring between her legs like he was. It was ludicrous, but he couldn't help feeling that way.

"Let me know when you start to feel a contraction coming on, hon. I'm going to check you while you're pressing down."

Gail didn't say anything. She was leaning back into Travis's lap as he held both of her hands in his. Her eyes were closed as she seemed to rest between the pain. It didn't last long.

"Here it comes," she managed to get out before groaning and clenching her teeth.

Travis urged her to breathe as she squeezed her eyes shut. Benton entered her with two fingers and felt around, trying to figure out what he was feeling. He couldn't tell anything at all, so he withdrew and wiped his slightly blood-tinged fingers on a bath towel to clean them.

"What did you figure out?" she demanded once the pain had passed."

"I can't feel the head, so you've still got a while before the birth. Let's make you as comfortable as possible in between contractions," he said.

"Comfortable? Are you freaking kidding me?"

* * * *

Gail fought the urge to curse as the contractions grew closer together. So far, the pain hadn't gotten any worse, just more frequent. It was wearing her down. She had a difficult time following the men's directions to pant and breathe through the pain. They needed to have the kind of pain she was having and try to breathe through it. Maybe then they'd understand.

She was so tired. She dozed between episodes only to come wide awake in an instant when one hit. Finally, after what seemed like days, Benton announced that he could feel the baby's head.

"You're nearly there, babe," Travis told her.

He'd changed positions so that his legs stretched straight out on either side of her body as she leaned back against his front. He never let go of her hands unless she pulled them away to dig into the bedding with her nails. Then he'd wipe her brow with a wet cloth. At some point, he'd pinned her hair up to get it off her back. It felt so much better without the wet strands sticking to the back of her neck.

"Move her down toward me a little, Travis. I want to be closer when the baby comes." Benton slid his hands beneath Gail's ass and pulled when Travis pushed. She moved about a foot before they stopped.

"How's that?" Travis asked.

"Much better. I don't want her to hang off the edge so the baby will be safe when he comes out. I just need to be a little closer." Benton patted Gail's thighs. "You're doing great, honey. Just a little longer."

A little longer stretched into an hour. She was ready to quit now. She didn't want to do this anymore. She was so very tired.

The next contraction hit her, and she cried out. "I can't stand this. Make it stop, Benton. Make it stop."

"I've got you, babe. Squeeze my hands and breathe." Travis rubbed his face against Gail's.

"The head's moving, hon. Push for me." Benton's voice seemed to come from a thousand miles away.

She pushed. Her body didn't seem to have the energy, but she did her best. She pushed until the contraction seeped away.

"The head is right there, honey. Just push once more, and I bet it will pop right through."

"You push. I can't do it anymore. I'm too tired, Benton. I'm just done."

The next contraction followed fast on the heels of the last. She all but sat up as pain burned around her middle. She groaned then bellowed out as she clamped down around her belly.

"Just like that, hon. Come on, Gail. Push hard. The head is just about through. That's right. I can see his face now. You got it!"

Where were they, a damn ball field? She gasped and panted as she tried to catch her breath again. That pain had been far worse. She felt as if she had a basketball between her legs now that had come out of her.

"Oh, God. I can't do that again." Gail squeezed her eyes shut as the next pain hit her.

"He's moving again. Push hard, Gail. Give him to me. Just a little more. Come on, hon. You can do it." Benton's urging voice barely reached her ears as the ringing in them out sang his words.

"I've got him. I've got him, Gail."

She coughed as she struggled to take a clear breath. Her body burned down there, and her belly ached like a son of a bitch. She closed her eyes and sank back for a second until she heard her baby cry. Gail's eyes snapped open.

"Is he okay? Let me see him. I need him, Benton. Give him to me." She reached forward with her arms but couldn't make herself sit up. Her abdomen was just too tired to obey.

"It's a girl, Gail. You gave us a perfect little girl. Hold on. I'm cleaning out her nose and mouth so she can breathe properly." Benton's voice sounded shaky.

Then he was laying her wet baby girl on her belly between her breasts as he rubbed a towel over her to clean her up.

"Look at what you did, babe. She's beautiful, Gail." Travis's voice was just as shaky as Benton's had been.

"Look at her little fingers. They're so tiny," Gail said as the baby's hand curled around her pinky.

"She has all ten of her fingers and toes," Benton said. "I counted."

"I can't believe she's finally here. What time was she born?" Gail asked.

"It was around two thirty in the morning, babe. I looked at my watch about the time Benton caught her." Travis looked over at the other man. "What about the cord. Did you clip it yet?"

"No. I just clamped it. I wanted to wait until I was sure the clamp was on right. I've got some twine in case we need to tie it off."

Gail cooed at her baby. The little girl was fussy, but not crying. She ignored whatever Benton was doing between her legs. She didn't want to think about it. All she cared about was her baby.

"So, did you choose between the names we agreed on?" Travis asked her.

"Grace. She's amazing Grace to me," she said.

"Perfect," Benton and Travis said at the same time.

"Let me finish cleaning her up, then you need to feed her, honey." Benton reached for her little angel, and Gail reluctantly released the child into his arms.

"We made a beautiful baby together," Travis said.

"Yes, we did. All three of us."

Chapter Nine

Gail sighed as she felt one of the men lay Grace over her chest and helped her sit up so that the baby could feed. She leaned against one while the other one rubbed her already distended nipple over her baby's mouth. The little tiger grabbed hold of it and began to suck as if she hadn't eaten just four hours earlier.

"Go on back to sleep, babe. We've got this," Travis said.

"I'll be glad when she sleeps through the night," Gail said with a mouth-stretching yawn.

"Won't be long, hon. We'll all be happy when that happens," he said with a chuckle.

"I'm sorry you guys keep getting up with her."

"Don't be. Sometimes it's just one of us, but we both woke up this time. We usually take turns, but it's just about time for us to get up anyway," Travis told her. "I'm going to go start the coffee then fix you something to eat before I go out to work in the garden."

"Let the wolves in for a second before you let them outside. I want to make sure they get used to Grace so they'll protect her like they protect me."

"I'll let them in for a few seconds. I don't want them to hurt you by accident," Travis told her.

"They won't. I think they're still pouting because you didn't let them in when I had her."

"I wasn't about to have four wolves in here while you gave birth," Benton said for the fifth time.

"I know, I know. Still." Gail still hadn't opened her eyes. She was still sleepy.

She heard the door open then the sound of nails on the floor near the bed. She felt the bed move as the wolves all propped themselves on the edges of the bed to sniff and whine at her and baby Grace. She opened her eyes a bit reluctantly but wanted to see her little wolves. They were all grown up now.

"Their tails are wagging like they'll fly right off. I think they're just as proud as we are, Benton," Travis said.

"I doubt that. I'm so proud my chest hurts," the other man said.

"Yeah, me, too." Travis whistled for the wolves to follow him.

They jumped down as if reluctant to leave, but followed Travis out before he shut the door behind him. Gail looked over at Benton, who was stroking one finger down their baby's back.

"She's so sweet. She only cries a little bit to get our attention, then she quiets the second we touch her," Benton said.

"I know. We're so lucky to have such an easy baby. There'll be plenty of times when she'll scream her head off like if she gets colic or something. I'm just going to enjoy this for as long as it lasts," she said.

"I don't want her to get sick. We'll be extra careful with her."

"You can't prevent colic, Benton. It's just something that happens sometimes. I've read all over the books we have, and nothing really cures it. Rubbing her belly and walking her helps, but it doesn't always." She sighed and changed baby Grace to her other breast.

Benton took a soft cloth and patted her nipple then held it there for a few seconds to absorb the leakage. When she looked over at him, he waggled his brows suggestively.

"Pervert."

"Can't help it. You've got great big boobs now. They're a man's fondest wish."

"I might even get to keep them once I finish breastfeeding," she told him.

"I can only pray."

Gail giggled then quieted when baby Grace's eyes opened to stare up at her. She adjusted her in the crook of her arm and sighed with contentment. She was so lucky to have this perfect little person as well as her amazing men. They were doing everything they could to make all of it easy on her when they still had the garden to take care of. For the last five weeks, they'd catered to her as she'd negotiated the world of taking care of an infant.

The baby slept in the baby bed in their room with the men taking turns getting up with her to help Gail feed her then putting her back to bed after burping her. It gave the other man time to rest before his turn. During the day, one of them would carry baby Grace downstairs while the other one would help her down. They'd set up a car seat that she could carry around by the handle when she wanted to move from one room to the other. They hadn't allowed her to carry anything for the first few weeks, but after she'd thrown a super temper tantrum, they'd relented and allowed her to cart the seat with her.

Now she spent the day taking care of and feeding Grace while making flatbread or making sandwiches for the men. She kept their tea pitchers full and rested in between. She wanted to sit out on the back porch, but they said it wasn't a good idea for the baby to be outside yet. She didn't argue.

One of the things she truly enjoyed was dressing her little girl up in one of the hundreds of outfits she had that fit. She'd gone through the dresser and removed all the little boy clothes and filled it with baby girl outfits. Each drawer held a different size. Right now, she was still in the infant sizes as she'd been a tiny little girl when she'd been born. They hadn't had scales to weigh her, but she was sure she was a little early since she'd only been sixteen inches in length.

It didn't matter. She was perfect in every way. Gail kept her with her no matter where she went. If she was in the kitchen, she had Grace on one of the upturned chairs in the baby carrier slash car seat. It fit perfectly between the chair legs and kept her off the floor. Gail was afraid to leave her on the table in case she moved and the carrier rocked off it.

The wolves split their time between her and the baby when Gail was busy working in the kitchen. Two would sit or lay on either side of the baby, and two would follow her as she puttered around doing little things that made her feel productive while the men were working so hard outside.

One of them would check on her about every hour. She poured them tea for him to carry out with him, then the other one would show up with the empty glasses an hour later.

"You know the wolves will let you know if something's wrong, Travis," she told him the next time he walked inside. "You don't need to come in every few minutes."

"We don't come in that often. Besides, how can they get out to let us know you need us?" he asked.

Gail looked over at Wolfie. "Go on outside, Wolfie."

The largest of the four stood and padded over to the back door. He stood up and used his paws to turn the knob then walked out on the porch before nudging open the screen door. He barked once. Gail grinned over at the gaping Travis.

"Come on back in, boy. You were great."

Travis's eyes widened as the wolf nosed the screen door open, walked back inside, and closed the back door by himself. He lay down at the door as if guarding it. Gail knew Travis had thought the wolves were well trained, but he really hadn't paid much attention to just how well trained they really were.

"That's amazing. I won't worry nearly as much now. Can't wait to tell Benton about this. He still isn't convinced they're not completely wild and have you fooled," Travis said.

"They'll protect me and Grace with their lives, Travis. I know it deep in my heart. They see us all as a pack, and Grace is the baby in it. You'll see. One day they'll prove their loyalty to us."

"As much as I hope you're right. I don't want there to ever come a day where we have to depend on them to do that." Travis kissed her soundly on the mouth. "Stay safe, babe. I'm going back outside to the garden. Send one of the wolves if you need us."

"Wait. Take another glass of tea out with you. I'm sure Benton will be thirsty by now." Gail poured two glasses.

Travis downed his and handed the empty one back to her before carrying the other with him. Wolfie stood and moved out of the man's way then returned to his place guarding the door.

"You're all perfectly good wolves. Don't let either man bother you. They're just overprotective of me and Grace. They like you, too." Gail gave each of them a good head rub then caught sight of Grace waking up and squelching up her face as if she were about to cry.

She reached over and pulled little Grace from the seat and checked her diaper. She needed a change, then it would be time to feed her again. Gail carried her to the couch where she kept all the supplies she needed so that she didn't have to take a chance climbing the stairs with the men outside. She changed Grace on the soft towel she kept on one end of the couch and tied up the dirty diaper in a bag for the men to carry out and bury later. Then she sat with baby Grace and fed her. This was her special time with her little girl. She loved watching her as she fed, and brushed her knuckles lightly across her tiny cheek.

"I love you so much, little Grace. The guys love you, too. They get all gooey eyed when they hold you. It's so cute. I try to keep them from making baby talk to you, but they can't help it. I want them to talk adult with you so you'll know how to talk sooner. Can't break them of the habit though. You'll just have to learn from me and ignore them."

Gail smiled down at her tiny angel until she was finished eating then burped her and rocked her to sleep before slipping her back in the carrier. Then she began making pot pies for supper. She couldn't wait until they had corn to give her something different to make their bread from. The flatbread out of flax and other plants had gotten old fast. She prayed the corn would produce enough for them to grind into grain.

The one thing she wished they had but didn't were cows. When Grace grew up past breastfeeding, she would need milk to grow strong bones. Maybe they'd find a cow wandering around. Hell, she'd settle for a goat, though goat's milk tasted funny. She remembered that from living on the farm before she'd found Benton and Travis.

By the time the men had returned, Gail had the pies ready and was holding Grace after having changed her. She couldn't wait for bath time. She loved sponging her off with the guys helping. It proved to be a bonding time for the three of them. Grace's pretty blue eyes followed them as they leaned over her. So far, she had light blue eyes with a dark tuft of hair on the top of her head.

Benton had wanted to put a bow on it, but she'd refused until Grace was older. She didn't want any chance the bow would hurt her soft spot. Benton had agreed, and that was the end of that for now. She had no doubt her poor baby would end up wearing bows as soon as she'd let the man put one on her. They adored her nearly as much as she did.

"How is the garden doing?" she asked.

"Damn good, but so is the grass. We're going to have to really work this thing until the ground freezes, or we'll end up with tons of it again next year. I'm hoping we can slowly work it so that in a few years we don't have nearly the trouble we're having now," Travis said.

"I hate that you're having to do it all by yourself. I want to help," she said.

"You can help some once we get ready to harvest. You'll have so much to do putting everything up, you should rest and enjoy your free time for now. We'll probably have to help you with the baby by then so you can get everything canned and whatever you need to do to it," Benton told her.

"The baby will be a good eight or nine weeks by the time you get the early part of the harvest. We'll just get a few tomatoes, some okra, and some squash to begin with," Travis said. "Then, by mid-July, it will really start coming in."

"I can't wait. I want to do something besides walk around entertaining myself while Grace is asleep," she told them.

"Don't worry. It won't be long now." Benton peered over at Grace who'd been watching them as they'd talked over her. "How is my little butterbean?"

"She's not a butterbean," Travis said. "She's a buttercup."

"She's a baby who doesn't need to hear your baby talk." Gail bent over and kissed her on the forehead. "Do you, Grace?"

Grace bubbled out a noise that didn't mean much of anything, but Gail chose to hear it as agreement. She nodded at the men.

"What?" Travis asked.

"She agreed."

"No, she did not. She burped," Benton said.

"She just gurgled," Travis added.

"Neither one of you have been around her as much as I have. She agreed with me. I know her baby talk." Gail smiled then pushed past them to finish setting the table. "Go wash up. It's time to eat."

The two men growled, rubbing their bellies, and disappeared into the living room. She poured tea then set the pies on a potholder after getting them out of the oven where she'd left them to keep the bugs off them. Even though it didn't work, it was good for storing food so that flies and gnats weren't flying around it.

The sound of stomping feet on the stairs alerted her that the men were on their way back down. Grace started cooing as if knowing her dads were close by. Gail walked over and kissed the baby.

"Crap, did we wake her up? We've got to learn not to be so noisy on the stairs," Benton said.

"No, she was already awake. However, you do need to learn to watch your mouth around her before she gets old enough to mimic you." Gail planted her hands on her hips. "And learn to walk softer for when she is sleeping."

"Goes both ways, babe. You can have a potty mouth when you're riled up," Travis pointed out.

"I'm working on it. I've learned to change 'damn' into 'drat' most times. Supper's ready. Let's eat. I'm starved." Gail sat next to Grace so she could watch her while she ate. Benton sat on the other side and Travis next to Gail.

They talked about the garden and what was about ready to pull or pick. Gail had cut up two tomatoes for them to eat with their meal that night. They tasted amazing. She couldn't wait for more to get ready. They'd have them every night. She'd already decided to cook squash and onions when there was enough squash for a meal.

After they'd finished eating and Gail had cleaned the kitchen, they sat in the living room talking until time for bed. The men took turns tending to baby Grace, enjoying the one-on-one time with her. It gave Gail a little time to just relax and not be on constant Grace duty for a couple of hours.

That night when they'd gotten Grace to sleep, Gail ran one hand down Benton's shaft then squeezed it at the base.

"What do you think you're doing?" he asked, stilling her hand with his.

"Seeing if you were interested in messing around. I want to make love, Benton."

"Babe, it's only been a little over five weeks. You're still healing," Travis said as he climbed into bed.

"Most doctors allow sex after six weeks. It's nearly that now. I want you and Benton. It's been long enough." She knew her lips were poked out in an exaggerated pout, but she couldn't help it.

First it had been because she was so far along. Now it was because she wasn't far enough along. They were killing her. She'd never have believed that they would willingly hold back on sex.

"Gail. Just a few more days. We don't want to hurt you," Benton said.

"You're hurting me now. I want to have sex. I want my men inside of me, making me feel like a sexy woman instead of a fat mommy." She finally got out what was really bothering her.

She felt fat and not the least bit sexy anymore. She had stretch marks and a flabby belly. Though her boobs were huge and heavy, the rest of her lacked sex appeal, and the men being reluctant to fuck her only made her feel even more undesirable.

"Oh, baby. You're not fat, and you're the sexiest woman alive. Don't think like that. Having our baby made you even more desirable to us. It takes time for your body to heal, and with all the work you have ahead of you with harvest and taking care of Grace, you'll lose whatever weight you're worried about in no time," Travis told her then kissed her lightly across the mouth.

"I don't care if you don't lose weight. I still love you just like you are, hon. You're even more special to us now that you've given us a special little girl to love and raise. Stop beating yourself up," Benton said.

"I need you. Please don't make me beg like this. We can be careful if you're worried about hurting me. I'll tell you if you do." Gail wasn't taking no for an answer. She wanted them.

"On one condition," Travis said, despite Benton's shaking head.

The other man cursed then huffed out a breath. Gail could tell he wasn't at all happy with Travis.

"What?" she asked, relief leaving her almost giddy.

"You let us set the pace, and only one of us will actually fuck you this time. One round of sex is more than enough for so soon after you've given birth." Travis motioned to Benton. "You take care of her. I'll help."

"What about you?" Gail asked.

"I'm going to jerk off to the sight of my woman and my best friend fucking. Next best thing to the real thing," he said.

"You could come in my mouth," she told him, unsure of why he wouldn't want a blow job.

"I know, but this way I get to watch without losing myself in your mouth. You always rob me of all control when you suck my dick, babe. This time is for you. I'll get my turn tomorrow or the next day."

"I love you, Travis."

"Back at you, babe."

Chapter Ten

Gail nearly screamed at the first touch of Benton's mouth on her sex. It had been so long since they'd even touched her down there. Her pussy was super sensitive with need and soaking wet at the idea of finally having one of her men inside of her.

"Easy, honey. Just let me make sure you're ready." Benton licked her slit again. "Hell, you're wet enough to soak through the bed sheets."

"I've been horny for nearly a week, Benton. I finally couldn't stand it any longer," she told him.

She sighed when he licked her clit while entering her with one finger. It wasn't nearly enough to satisfy her, but she bit her tongue to keep from demanding more. She would be patient so that they didn't stop altogether.

Gail looked over to where Travis knelt back on his heels and pulled at his swollen cock with one hand held tightly around the shaft. She reached out to touch him. She could barely brush her fingertips over his tight balls.

"Easy, Gail. I don't want to come until you're ready. I'm barely holding on as it is," Travis said.

"Honey. Do you think you're ready for me? You're soaking wet," Benton said.

"Yes. I'm ready, Benton. Don't make me wait. Fill me up." Gail reached with both hands toward him.

"Damn, you're hot. I love how you want me like this, all desperate and needy." Benton guided his cock to her slick slit before slowly entering her while holding himself off her with one hand planted on the bed.

Gail sighed when he was seated all the way inside of her. It seemed like it had taken hours instead of mere seconds for him to completely fill her with his cock. She moaned when he slowly pulled back then pushed back in again.

"Faster, Benton. Don't tease me like this."

"Calm down, hon. I'm going to go faster once I'm ready. You need to be patient."

Gail huffed out a breath and reached out to Travis. She raked her nails lightly over his balls again. She needed something, and neither man was willing to give it to her right then. She watched as Travis squeezed the base of his dick then pulled on it until his fist covered the tip of him and rolled over the drop of pre-cum that gathered at the slit. She opened her mouth and stuck out her tongue.

"You want a taste?" Travis asked.

"Please. Just a little on my tongue," she said.

He swiped his finger across the tip then fed his finger to her. She licked at it and sucked it deep into her mouth. Perfect. He was salty and a little bitter, but he was Travis, one of her men. She liked every part of him.

"Was that good, hon? Did you like sucking Travis's cum?" Benton asked as he entered her a little harder this time.

"Yes," she wheezed out before arching her back to meet Benton's thrusts. "It was so good. This is so good."

"I love seeing you suck his dick. Maybe in a few days you can suck mine while he fucks you. Would you like that, Gail?" Benton asked.

"Yes! I want to suck your cock, Benton. I want Travis deep inside of me when I do. I can't wait until we can do double again. I've missed having you both in me at one time."

"It won't be long now, babe," Travis said. "Just another month or two. That's too hard on you so soon after you've had a baby. Let everything get back to normal inside of you first."

"Months? God, Travis. I can't wait that long." Gail gasped when Benton thrust deep and hard inside of her. "Oh, yes. That feels so good, Benton."

She moaned as he continued to tunnel in and out of her needy cunt with his thick dick. She moved with him, occasionally looking over to see what Travis was doing. He was jerking on his dick as if he would pull it off. When the men jacked off, they were so much harder than she could be. Gail didn't understand why it didn't hurt the way they tugged on themselves like they did.

Benton reached between them and fingered her clit as she groaned at the first waves of her impending orgasm that rolled through her body. She could feel her body tighten all over just waiting for her to go over. His pounding cock sent quivers down her spine as her ass muscles clenched, waiting, waiting for her climax to roll over her.

She heard Travis shout as he came and felt warm jets of his release land on her belly. That was all she needed to explode. She knew she took Benton with her as he jerked inside of her and slowed his pace when he came. Gail arched her back, taking all of him inside of her before she lay still, panting with the effort to breathe.

She was certain Benton was saying something as he lay over her, but she couldn't hear through the ringing in her ears. When he rolled off her and cupped her cheek in one hand, she strained to hear what he was saying.

"Are you okay? Did I hurt you, honey?"

"I'm great. Just trying to catch my breath," she told him.

"When you didn't answer me, I thought I'd hurt you," he explained.

"Can't hear well over the ringing in my ears." Gail reached up and touched his lips. "That was wonderful. Thank you."

"No need for thanks. I got mine, too, you know." He grinned down at her then rolled over and groaned.

"I'll bring back a wet cloth and clean you up, babe. I need to do a little cleaning myself." Travis grinned over at her when she turned his way.

"Thanks. I don't think I can move right now," she admitted.

"No need. I've got this." Travis climbed off the bed and disappeared into the darkness of the room.

"I love you, Gail. I don't care what you look like or how big you might get. I'll always love you because of who you are," Benton said in a soft voice. He threaded his fingers with hers and held her hand to his heart. "You're my everything, hon. Always and forever."

Gail felt tears burn the back of her eyes. "I love you, too, Benton. You make me feel special when I've never felt that way in my life before."

Travis appeared out of the gloom with a cloth in his hand. He quickly cleaned her belly then wiped between her legs so that she wouldn't feel so sticky in the morning. She started to get up, but Travis pressed her back down.

"I'll check on lady Grace. You rest. If she needs you, I'll bring her to you."

"Thanks, Travis. Love you," she said.

"Love you, too, babe. Go to sleep."

* * * *

"Just for a little while, babe. You and Grace can sit outside for an hour at most," Travis said several weeks later. "I don't want you to get overheated."

"We won't. I want to look at the garden. I haven't been out in it since it first started growing. Now it's all grown up, and you're bringing me things to put up. Please, Travis. Benton." Gail gave them what she hoped was her best puppy-dog expression.

"Dammit, Gail." Benton looked over at the sleeping Grace. "See, you're making me swear in front of the baby."

"I'm not making you do anything. Now stop fussing with me and just let me look around. The wolves will sit right here with Grace and watch over her while I walk around. I'm not going to do anything, just look."

"Fine," Benton said. "But you're going back inside at the first sign either of you look hot."

Gail smiled and kissed him on the mouth before turning to check on Grace. She patted the wolves' heads and walked toward the garden with Sasha following close behind. She explored the rows and noted what was close to being ready and what was ready to pull. She behaved herself and didn't try to pick anything, but would make sure the guys knew she'd found vegetables that needed to be picked.

The tomatoes were out of hand and overflowing with ripe ones. The peppers were nearly as full. The beans weren't quite ready, but the okra and squash were. She finally made it over to where the corn was planted in four long rows. The ears weren't quite filled out, but the plants were tall and had several ears on each one.

"What do you think?" Travis asked, catching up with her.

"It's wonderful. You and Benton have done an amazing job of keeping up despite helping me with Grace. How will you know when the potatoes and onions and garlic are ready?" she asked.

"By the way the plants begin to dry. We'll probably harvest all the root crops last except for the occasional onion for cooking with now. The garlic we'll hang in the cellar to dry it, and the onions and potatoes we'll put in the drying boxes down there for when we need them." Travis grasped her hand in his. "Did you see those tomatoes? You're going to spend all your time putting them up. I don't think there's any way you can keep up with the way they're producing."

"I'm going to do my best. What about the basil and mint? How is it doing? I didn't see any of it."

"It's fine. It's on the other side of the corn, so it would get a little shade from the sun in the afternoons. We'll dry it all for you to use for flavoring. It might taste pretty good to have a little mint in our tea from time to time," he said.

"Thanks for letting me walk around some. I needed out of the house. I've been cooped up inside of there for nearly three months now. It's time for me to move around in the fresh air," Gail told him.

"I know, babe, but Benton's right. You tend to try to go too fast, and we've got to be the voice of reason at times. You've got all the time in the world. Enjoy the peace and quiet while you have it. It won't be long until baby Grace starts growing up and keeping you on your toes." Travis kissed the top of her head.

"Hey, that's keeping all of us on our toes. You guys are going to have Grace duty just like I do," she said, narrowing her eyes.

Travis laughed. "I know, I know. Come on. It's time to go inside. Your face is a little pink from the sun. Benton will have a cow if you get sunburned out here."

"Fine. It's about time for me to feed Grace anyway. This had been fun. I'll work on canning tomatoes after I feed her. You need to get to work picking them for me." She shook a finger at him.

"I hear you, boss," Travis said.

"Hear what?" Benton asked as he joined them on the walk back to where Grace and the wolves were.

"You left Grace alone with the wolves?" she asked with a mock frown.

"Only for as long as it took to meet you and walk you back. Even I can tell that they'd fight anything that gets near her. I'm almost afraid to go over there without you to shield me," he muttered.

Gail laughed. She loved her men. They were so different but worked together perfectly. Benton with his overprotectiveness reminded her of the wolves, while Travis was fun loving and often the one to bring Benton out of the clouds when he got to be too much for her.

"See, she's fine," Benton said.

Sasha padded over to the baby and sniffed before sitting down next to Wolfie, who seemed to have sentry duty next to the carrier that was sitting on an upturned chair for safety. Both Gigi and Max lay around the chair to keep all danger at bay. Her wolves were amazing.

"I'll carry Grace inside for you, hon." Benton walked over, eyeing Wolfie and Sasha warily, to pick up the carrier. "Travis, move the chair back to the porch, will you?"

"Got it," Travis said.

Gail followed Benton inside with the wolves in a line behind her. She heard Travis talking to Max who was at the rear of the line. It made her smile. He treated them like pets more so than Benton did, but she could tell that Benton was a little more relaxed around them than he'd been at first.

"Need any help getting her settled?" Benton asked.

"Nope. I'm going to feed her, then I'll start on the tomatoes. Why don't you and Travis pick all of the ripe ones, so I can get started on them?" she asked.

"We will. Don't overdo it though. You can always work on them tomorrow. They won't ruin for several days, Gail." Benton kissed her before leaving her to carry Grace to the living room where she normally sat on the couch to feed her little munchkin.

She settled Grace at her breast and thought over what she'd do first. After shifting her to the other breast, Gail had a plan mapped out in her head of where to start. The hardest part was cooking the tomatoes over the fire without scalding them then sealing the jars with hot water boiling over the fire.

Grace pulled free of her breast and looked up at her with a puzzled expression. Gail laughed at her. She always looked that way until Gail burped her. This time was no different. She settled a burp cloth over one shoulder, hiked her little girl up, and began patting her on the back in soft even strokes. After two large belches, Gail cradled her in her arms and sang to her until her eyes closed and she relaxed in her mother's arms.

Gail settled her in the car seat then washed the tomatoes before putting them in a bowl to carry into the living room to transfer into the large boiler to boil so she could remove the peelings easier. Then they'd only need another thirty minutes to cook before she sealed them in jars.

By the time the men returned from working all day in the garden, Gail had managed to put up nearly twenty-six jars of tomatoes. She had another boiler of tomatoes she'd mashed into sauce boiling on the fire along with a pot of rabbit stew she'd made from some of the dried rabbit meat from the last time they'd killed one.

"After you wash up, we can eat. I have some stew and flatbread and a couple of tomatoes cut," she told them.

"How are you doing?" Benton asked before walking off.

"I'm good. Being outside in the fresh air and sunshine really helped," she told him.

"Your face is a little pink. Did you get burned?" he asked.

"I don't burn. I tan. I'm sure it's from working over the fire so much this afternoon," she told him then pushed him toward the stairs. "Go wash up. Even if you're not hungry, I am."

"I'm going. Just wanted to be sure you hadn't overdone it. We'll help you with the last of the canning tonight," he said.

"Nope. You'll relax in your recliners and snooze. I only have six or seven jars to put up. It won't take more than another thirty or forty-five minutes after we eat."

Benton sighed and shook his head. She could hear him muttering about her being a stubborn woman as he walked off. She let it pass. She was a stubborn woman and proud of it. Sometimes being stubborn is what got you what you wanted. It wouldn't be long before what she wanted was both men, inside of her at one time. Then she'd get her stubborn on like nothing they'd ever seen before.

Chapter Eleven

August hung heavy in the air with the scent of fall in the falling leaves and decaying vegetation. The one thing that made it all better was that harvest was coming to an end soon, and she'd be able to relax with her baby and contemplate more time with her men. Once the first frost came, they could clean out the garden and ready it for winter. She looked forward to that with all her heart and her tired aching fingers.

Gail stood and rubbed her aching back. She'd been picking peas for nearly an hour, and so far, Grace hadn't once made a noise that she wanted out of the playpen or needed changing. The wolves had her completely enclosed in their watchful circle. Baby Grace was nearly four months old now. She was already showing signs of being able to flip from her back to her tummy. It wouldn't be long before she'd be pulling herself up and saying her first words.

The soft cooing noises she made when one of the guys held her had them making all kinds of faces and baby noises back at her. Gail couldn't break them of the habit and had finally given up. She'd talk to little Grace like an adult and make sure she knew how to say "mama" and "dada" early.

"Hey, Gail. We're going to run down to the stream and try some fishing. This may be one of the last days we might be able to have fish for supper," Travis said.

"Go ahead. I'll call or send one of the wolves to get you if I need anything," she told him. "Grace is keeping the wolves entertained, and I'm nearly to the end of this row of beans. We'll probably go inside after that."

"Just leave the playpen out here, and we'll carry it in when we get back. If we don't catch something quick, we won't bother trying any longer. They might not bite with the cooler weather heading in."

"Tell Benton I love him. Love you, too, Travis."

"Love you back, knucklehead."

Gail smiled at the endearment. He was always coming up with names for her and poor Grace. He'd taken to calling her Gracie and munchkin despite her insistence that they use her real name. Benton had even started her calling her princes. The poor child wouldn't know her real name at the rate they were going.

She shook her head, and after one last look at her baby, she buried her head in the plants and continued picking.

A noise somewhere in the woods at her back made her stand up and listen. She thought she heard something, but the wolves weren't paying in attention to that area of the yard. The wind was blowing in that direction, so they might not be able to smell anything. After several seconds, she didn't hear anything again, so she ignored her gut that something was out there.

She'd just reached the end of the row when the wolves began growling and barking at something behind her. She turned around to see a giant bear, a grizzly it looked like, running in the direction of the wolves—and her baby. She screamed and ran toward the bear to stop it. The growling tower of fur stood up and roared back at her. It looked from the wolves back to her then the wolves once more. Gail screamed for Travis and Benton as loud as she could, but fear clogged her throat, making it nearly impossible to get anything out.

Gail grabbed the hoe lying at the end of the row and began waving it at the bear. She saw Gigi jump inside the playpen and grab baby Grace in her mouth and jump back out only to run toward the porch. Gail didn't see what happened after that since the bear started attacking the wolves that were jumping at it from all sides.

Gail tried to run around the bear to get to her baby, but it blocked her path each time. She winced each time it swiped at one of the wolves, sending it flying, but they kept getting up and attacking the creature, trying to give her a clear path to the house. She screamed at the grizzly, making nonsense cries to try and scare it away, but only the hoe and the wolves kept it from reaching her.

Where were the guys? Surely, they'd heard her by now. It wasn't all that far from the stream. Had something happened to them? Had the bear already gotten to them? Gail's mind raced despite her battle with the huge animal.

The more she fought, the more tired she got so that it was getting harder and harder to use the hoe on the wild beast. The wolves didn't seem to lose their resolve to kill or at least scare away the big monster. She thought about her baby with Gigi, and a new gush of anger tinged fear spurred her on once again. She managed to cut into the bear several times, but it didn't seem to do anything but enrage it more.

Please, God. Don't let it get my baby. I don't understand where the guys are. Why haven't they come? They always come when I call them.

Gail tried once again to move around the beast, but it shifted with her, only taking the time to swipe at one of the wolves when it got too close. She thought about turning and running toward the stream, but knew the bear would easily overtake her before she could reach the men. If they were even still alive. They had to be alive. Anything else would kill her as surely as the bear.

* * * *

Travis had just tossed his hook in the stream when he heard a noise that sounded like a moo. He listened but couldn't hear anything more over the sound of the water rushing over the rocks.

"Did you hear something?" he asked Benton who'd walked several yards farther down the bank of the stream.

"No. What did it sound like?"

"I could have sworn I heard a moo."

"Like a cow?" Benton stared at him. "Are you going crazy or something?"

"I swear it sounded like a cow mooing."

Benton cocked his head as if listening then shook it. "I don't hear anything. Must have been something in the wind."

Travis sighed and watched his cork for any sign that he'd snagged a fish. He sure hoped they managed to catch something. It would be great to have fish for supper. He didn't even mind cleaning them if they actually caught one or two. If they only got one, they'd let Gail have it. She deserved everything they could give to her.

Once again, a mooing noise reached his ear. This time when he turned toward Benton, the other man seemed to have heard it, too. He was looking around them.

"You heard it, too. Can you tell which direction it's coming from?" Travis asked.

"No, with the noise of the stream it's hard to tell. I'll go across the stream and see if it's louder over there. You stay there and listen." Benton pulled his line in and dropped it on the ground before pulling off his boots and wading into the stream to cross to the other side.

He ended up thigh-deep before he reached the middle. By the time he made it to the other side, Travis had heard the animal twice more. He still wasn't sure where it was coming from.

"Do you hear it over there?" he shouted.

"Yeah! It's on this side. Wait there and I'll see if I can find it. No use in you getting all wet if I can grab it myself."

Travis doubted the cow could be coerced by one man to cross the water without kicking up a fuss. He didn't argue with him, just waited for him to return and tell him he needed help. After about five minutes, Benton returned empty-handed with a scowl on his face.

"You're going to have to come help me. She's shy of me and has a calf, as well. Grab the rope out of the bag I was carrying. It might be long enough to go around her neck. The calf will follow wherever she goes, I think," he said.

Travis pulled in his empty hook and stashed it inside the bag after pulling out the rope. There wasn't much to it, but it should be enough to wrap around the cow's neck and tug on it. At least he hoped it would be. Getting a cow would be wonderful with Gail and the baby. They'd have fresh milk every day. Their child would need milk to grow up strong.

He pulled off his boots and waded into the still warm water and crossed to where Benton stood holding out his hand to help him up the bank. He followed his friend to find the cow and its calf grazing on grass in a small open area between towering trees. When Benton moved in its direction, it moved a few feet in the opposite direction.

"See what I mean?"

"I'll circle around to the other side and we'll box it in. One of us should be able to grab hold of it until the other can help rope it."

Benton nodded. "I'll wait on you before I move again. We sure don't want to spook it into running."

Travis walked wide of the cow to the other side then started to inch his way toward the animal in hopes it wouldn't notice until he'd made it closer. Benton didn't move for several moments then followed suit.

Together they managed to nearly reach the cow before it looked up. They froze and looked at the ground, waiting for the heifer to go back to eating grass. The calf didn't give them a single glance as it ate. It was at least five or six months old. A good age to follow its mom wherever she went.

Travis reached the cow when it looked over at Benton. He tossed the rope over its neck having already worked into a loose noose. When it started to walk away, it stopped with the slight tug of the rope and looked at Travis as if he'd done something strange. The fact that it didn't fight the rope gave him some hope that they'd manage to return to the house without a struggle.

It all went fine until they reached the stream that was washing loudly over the rocks. The cow balked. Benton and Travis had to yell at each other to be heard over the den of the mooing cow and the noise of the water. Finally, they managed to get both the cow and the calf across the stream, though both he and Benton ended up soaked to the bone from head to toe. When they reached the other side, they took turns holding the cow by the rope while they put on their boots. Despite their socks being wet, they couldn't walk back to the house without them.

"Fucking cow. I hope she makes a lot of milk after all of this," Benton grumbled.

"For fresh milk for Gracie, it's all worth it," Travis said.

"Yeah. You're right." Benton followed them as Travis tugged on the rope to get the cow going again.

Benton had to walk behind the calf to be sure it didn't wander off as they neared the house. It was then that they heard the most spine-ripping screams he'd ever heard. Travis dropped the rope of the cow and sprinted off toward the house with Benton close behind him.

When they reached the garden, they could hear the wolves growling and yapping with Gail's screeches and the sounds of a wild animal bellowing at the top of its lungs. Travis couldn't tell what was going on. He shoved his way through the garden, jumping over plants and pushing through others. What he saw when he broke free was enough to send his heart into spasms.

Gail stood with Max and Sasha on one side and Wolfie on the other side of a huge grizzly. They were all lashing out at it, Gail with a hoe. She had blood all over her, but he couldn't tell whose it was since all of them were covered in blood, including the bear.

He and Benton grabbed weapons that lay around the garden. He had the digging fork, and Benton grabbed a shovel. The three of them beat at the bear, tearing into it until he didn't know how it was standing.

Gail broke free and ran for the house. He prayed that Gracie was inside since he didn't see the baby in the playpen. By the time they had the bear beat back, it turned and limped away with the wolves chasing it into the woods, leaving Travis and Benton frantic to find Gail and Gracie.

When they burst inside, Gail was on the floor hugging the baby to her, and Gigi stood between them growling until she realized it was them. Then she returned to Gail, rubbing her chin all over her head making little nipping sounds.

"Oh, honey." Benton dropped to his knees next to her. "Are you okay? What about Grace?"

Gail's crying got even louder as she tried to talk through it. "I'm fine. Grace is fine."

She gulped then broke into loud wails again. Travis didn't know what to do other than hug her with Benton.

"If it wasn't for the wolves, we'd all be dead. The bear came out of nowhere and got between me and Grace." She sniffed and swallowed as if trying to control her breathing. "I couldn't get to Grace, and the bear turned toward her. I grabbed the first thing I saw and attacked it. The wolves all jumped in and helped me."

"Easy, babe. We've got you and Grace is fine. Are you sure you're not hurt?"

"I don't think so. The wolves kept between me and the bear as much as they could. I know they're hurt. Where are they?" She looked around then down at Gigi. "Gigi jumped in the playpen and grabbed Grace by her clothes then carried her in the house. I couldn't believe what I was seeing, then all I could do was fight the bear. It wouldn't let me get to the house."

"It's all over now, babe. Try to catch your breath and let us look over you and Grace." Travis pulled back and felt her face then down each arm as Benton pulled a wailing Grace from her mother's arms.

"You've got some cuts on your hands and arms, Gail. Come on and stand up so I can check the rest of you." Travis tugged at her until she stood.

"Benton? Is Grace really okay? Did you check her?" Gail asked.

"She's fine. She has a tiny cut on the back of her shoulder. I'm sure one of Gigi's teeth nipped it by accident. I'm surprised she doesn't have a lot of them. That damn wolf is a hero." Benton rubbed the wolf's fur. "Hell, they all are. I'll never complain about them again."

"I don't see anything else other than what's on your hands and arms. The bear got you pretty good there, babe. We need to clean you up and take care of them so they don't get infected." Travis eased her over to a chair and urged her to sit.

"The wolves. Where are they?" she asked, looking around.

"I'll check on them later," Travis told her.

"No. I need them here with me. They saved our lives," she insisted.

Grace had settled down now that Gail had stopped crying. Benton looked at Travis and nodded then settled the baby in her seat.

"I'll go check on them and be right back." Benton walked out of the door after getting an ax to carry with him.

"I'm so sorry we didn't hear you, babe." Travis got a wet cloth and began to clean the worst of her cuts.

"Where were you?"

"The stream is really loud now that it's rushing over the rocks since the water level's gotten so low. Then we heard what sounded like a cow and crossed to the other side to find out it was a cow. That's why we didn't hear you. I'm so sorry, babe. It will never happen again. We won't ever leave you alone like that again. One of us will always be near you." Travis couldn't believe they'd nearly lost their woman and baby over a stupid cow.

He shook his head. Even now that cow was probably wandering off with the rope around its neck. Travis rinsed out the cloth, pink with her blood, and started on the other arm.

"None of these are too deep, but you've got two that really need stitches, Gail. Once I've got them all clean, we're going to have to sew those two up. They won't heal well if we don't."

"After having a child and fighting a bear, I think I can handle a few stitches," she said with a watery smile. She shifted to look over at Grace again.

"She's sleeping. After all that's happened, she's sleeping like an angel," Travis assured her.

"I couldn't get to her, Travis. What would have happened if Gigi hadn't saved her?"

"Don't think about it. It didn't happen and won't happen. We'll make sure of it."

"How? You can't protect us twenty-four hours a day. We have to work, and that means we're separated sometimes. I wish we still had guns with bullets. I know what I need. I need some spears. That would help." Gail looked up at him with a determined glint in her eye. "We can make spears, right? Like how you made those arrows."

"We can do that. It will give you some protection just in case something happens that separates us again. We'll teach you how to throw them, too," he said.

"I don't ever want to feel helpless like that again."

"We won't let you. We'll make sure you know how to use the spear and how to shoot the bow and arrow. Then you can protect yourself and the baby."

"When the Grace gets old enough, we're teaching her, too," she demanded.

"We'll teach her, too."

The door opened, and the wolves all poured in, circling around them, sniffing Gail then Gracie then Gail again. They whined and yipped but appeared mostly unscathed.

"Are they okay?" Gail asked Benton.

"Yeah. Wolfie has a good-sized scratch on his side, but it doesn't look too bad. If he'll let us, we'll try sewing it, but it might do better without stitches. Sasha has a few scratches across her back quarters, but they aren't even as deep as Wolfie's. Max seemed to get the least of the wounds with some scratches across his nose and one side of his neck." Benton looked her over. "You need stitches, too."

"Yeah, Travis told me. Is the bear gone?"

"Actually, it's dead. The wolves finished it off. They were guarding the body, I think. I guess we should try and cut up some of it and put it in the fridge for food for them and us."

"You do that. I want to eat that damn bear even if it doesn't taste good," Gail said with enough anger in her voice to widen Benton's eyes.

"Why don't you look for that cow first? Just in case it's still around somewhere," Travis suggested. "Milk would taste good with bear."

Benton snorted. "I wish we'd never heard that damn cow. We might have heard Grace screaming if we hadn't been across the river."

"Maybe. Maybe not. I hadn't realized just how loud it was down there until we started trying to listen for the noise we heard." Travis shook his head as he cleaned the last scratch on her hand.

"I'll check for the cow first then see about that bear. Don't leave them for anything while I'm gone," Benton said.

"You don't have to tell me. I'm glued to her side until you get back. I've got to sew up these cuts so they'll stop bleeding. We'll attempt to sew up Wolfie's when you get back."

"I'm really looking forward to that," Benton said with a wince.

"Be careful, Benton. Don't look for the cow too long. I'd rather you came back here where you're safe," Gail said.

She reached out and squeezed the other man's hand before laying her head against Travis's shoulder. He'd protect her and the baby with his life. He'd nearly lost them. Nothing would ever erase the sight of her fighting that grizzly for as long as he lived.

Chapter Twelve

Gail lay on the couch with her head in Benton's lap and her feet on Travis's. Her arms ached where Travis had sewn them up the day before, but they weren't bad. Mostly she was sore from hitting the tough old bear with the garden hoe. It had sounded all the way up her arms into her shoulder each time she'd made contact. Now she felt as if her entire body had taken a beating.

Baby Grace was asleep, lying on her chest, and the wolves were all lying around the floor in front of the couch. They'd eaten bear the night before, and despite her determination to hate the taste of it, the beast hadn't been all that bad. They had roast simmering in the Dutch oven on the fire now. She'd added potatoes, onions, and a fourth of a clove of garlic to season it some.

Benton had managed to find the stupid cow and her calf wandering around on the other side of the garden, and they were now living inside the shed. They planned to build a lean-to next to the shed to house most of the garden tools, so the entire shed could house the cow and her calf. They'd need to enlarge it after winter to accommodate two full-grown cows. That wouldn't be easy with planting a garden to do, as well.

Gail knew their lives were about to get even more complicated now that they had a baby, two cows, the garden, and the need to trap or kill for meat. Where once there'd only been the three of them, now there was much more. The wolves figured into the mix as mostly self-sufficient, but an integral part of their safety as well as their lives.

"Whatcha thinking about, babe?" Travis asked as he massaged her feet.

"Just thinking about how much our lives have changed and will change over the winter," she said.

"What do you mean?" Benton asked as he twirled her hair around his finger.

"Well, we have a growing baby girl now as well as the four wolves. Add to that a cow and her calf and growing a garden and harvesting it and killing for meat, and there's not a lot of room for times like this," she told them.

"We'll always make times for this, hon. This is what makes it all worthwhile," he said.

Travis squeezed her foot. "We'll make time even when it seems like we don't have it to take."

"I hope so. I love laying here between the two of you with Grace. We almost lost us yesterday. I don't want to ever take any of us for granted. Okay?" She looked from one to the other.

"Never, babe."

"Never." Benton brushed a kiss across her forehead.

"I think supper's ready if you guys are," she said. "I just need to set the table and get it off the fire."

"We'll set the table and take it all into the kitchen for you. Just lie here for a little while longer with Grace. Then we'll put her in her seat and eat," Travis said.

She nodded and lifted her feet so he could get up then sat up a little bit so that Benton could, as well. He shoved a pillow behind her head so she would be comfortable before he walked over to the fire to lift the heavy Dutch oven off the pole with the heavy-duty oven mitts. Once he'd left the bear roast in the kitchen, he returned for the boiler of peas. She watched him walk back into the kitchen and couldn't help but admire his tight ass. Her men had hot hard bodies from all the work they did outside.

Gail was surprised she'd feel the way she did right then. She hadn't been able to sleep the night before, wanting to check on Grace every few minutes, but she'd had several nice naps during the day and was feeling strongly the need to have her men.

Together.

In bed.

Nearly losing everything had made it clear to her that she had to take what she wanted every chance she got. She would savor the little moments and paste them to her heart so that she'd never forget them. Not just Grace's first moments, but all of their moments together, the three of them. They all mattered when everything could be swept away with a storm, a fire, or a bear.

"Supper's on the table, babe. I'll take Grace." He reached and picked up the sleeping baby then held out one hand to help her up.

Grace yawned and opened her eyes to peer into Travis's. She cooed then made a popping sound with her mouth. Gail couldn't help but giggle at the cute little trick she'd taught herself. She'd been making popping noises for several days now. Each time she did it, little Grace grinned and did it again.

"She's so damn cute," Travis said.

"Language."

"Oops. Sorry. But she is."

"I know."

Benton took Grace from Travis's arms and cooed to her before settling her in her seat at the table. She lay there looking up at the makeshift mobile Benton had fashioned and hung from the ceiling just for her. It held feathers, a bear claw, some pretty pieces of cloth, and a small antler from one of the younger deer they'd killed last winter. She waved her arms at it then farted and giggled again.

"That's a lovely sound to eat supper over," Travis said with a chuckle.

"Just pray there's no smell with it, or the wolves will drive us crazy until we change her," Benton said.

Gail couldn't help but laugh at them. This was her family and they were all perfect.

* * * *

"Someone's horny," Travis said with a snort when Gail reached around him from the back and grasped his cock with both hands.

"Umhum."

"Sure you feel up to a little hanky-panky?" he asked.

"I wouldn't be hinting if I weren't."

"Hinting at what?" Benton walked out of the bathroom after switching off the light.

"At needing both of you. Inside me. Now." Gail let go of Travis and sauntered over to Benton. She rubbed against his chest with hers then stroked his engorged cock with one hand and gently rolled his balls with the other. "Understand?"

"I think I've got the picture."

"Good. I hate having to spell it out. Makes me think you don't want me if I have to do that." Gail released her hold on Benton and walked over to the bed where she crawled up the middle, putting an extra sway to her hips as she did.

"Fuck. Look at that ass," Benton said.

"I'm looking, I'm looking." Travis walked over to his side of the bed and sat.

"I've got her sweet ass this time," Benton said.

"No problem. I want inside that wet pussy," Travis said.

"Boys, boys. Stop talking and start playing." Gail lifted her ass as she held herself up on her knees and hands.

Travis rolled over to slip beneath her so that she was hovering over his hard body. She loved running her hands up and down her men's chests and abdomens. While they had good definition, they weren't bodybuilders. They were hard workers. She loved every square inch of their sexy bodies. She especially loved squeezing their asses every chance she got. They were tight and round, just like she liked them.

Now she traced Travis's nipple with her tongue then lapped at the other one. His quick intake of breath told her he enjoyed what she did. She kissed her way across his wide chest before moving north to lick and nip at his neck.

"Give me that mouth, babe. I want to taste you." Travis grasped her head in his hands and drew her down so that he could kiss her.

Gail loved it when her men took her kisses. They mastered her mouth and tangled their tongues with hers. The taste of Travis went to her head as he stole her breath then her sanity with how her breasts felt rubbing against his sprinkling of chest hair. They stimulated her nipples to the point of near pain. She needed her breasts touched, tasted. They ached for her men's touch.

"Easy, babe. We've got you." Travis kissed the corners of her mouth then guided her over his hard, hot cock until her slit lined up it.

She sank down, encasing the long length of him with her wet pussy. It felt so good to finally have him inside of her. Gail rode him as she guided his hands from her hips to her breasts. He mounded them then gently tugged on the nipples. They leaked milk, but neither of the men minded. It was all part of their woman, they'd told her.

After she and Travis had messed around for a while, Benton pushed her down to lay on Travis's chest so that he could prepare her for his dick.

"Just relax, honey. I want it to be good for you, so I need to get you ready."

"Please hurry, Benton. I need you inside of me."

"I've got you. Be still for a few minutes for me." Benton rubbed the greasy lube they used across her ass then squeezed more directly over her back hole.

She sighed as he played with her ass, dipping his finger in the little hole until he was able to sink his entire finger deep inside. Then he added more of the gel and a second finger. She moaned as the initial ache turned into a burn that she relished. She knew that after he pumped his fingers in and out for a few seconds, he'd add more lube, then his rock-hard cock would come next.

"Now, Benton. I need you now." She loved to tease him by pushing back against him when he was trying to go slow and prepare her.

"Be still, hon. I don't want to hurt you."

Benton pulled out his fingers then added the extra lubricant before pressing the tip of his thick dick into her back hole. It burned and pinched until he got past the tight ring that tried to keep him out. Once he'd managed to get inside, he stilled for a few precious seconds that she tried to remain still while he regained his control. Finally, she couldn't stand it any longer. She pushed back on him then pulled off so that she rode Travis's cock deeper. Benton caught on and moved her between them. One second she'd be all the way down on his stiff shaft, then he'd push her nearly all the way off so that she took in all of Travis's, long rod.

"Fuck, your ass is tight, hon. I'm never able to hold on very long when I'm inside you back here."

"Doesn't matter if it's her ass or her cunt," Travis said. "She wipes me out in only a few minutes."

"I bet that wet pussy feels like a velvet fist," Benton teased his friend.

"Fuck yeah. She's squeezing me every time you push her down on me. Just for a second when we're both inside her, I swear my eyes cross at how good it feels. She's so damn wet and hot and tight."

"Same here, man."

Gail couldn't think at all as they moved her back and forth, until she saw stars as her climax rode her hard. She started to scream but clamped down to keep from waking the baby. That sucked. She really needed to scream.

"I wish you could see her right now, Benton. She's coming, and her face is fucking beautiful." Travis shoved his dick inside her, then cursed as he filled her with his cum.

Gail could feel every drop of it, then felt Benton do the same. Both men cursed under their breath. They'd all learned their lesson about screaming and shouting during sex. It made for a rude ending to what had been amazing before little Grace woke up crying.

"I can't breathe," Travis said in a pinched voice. "Get the fuck off Gail, man. You weigh a ton."

"Do not." Benton panted around his words.

"Don't argue and wake up Grace, or you'll both be sleeping downstairs in your recliners tonight," Gail whispered. She was fighting to regain her own breath after that.

They both winced and shut up. She knew that neither one of them wanted to sleep anywhere but with their woman and their baby with them. She secretly prayed that Grace wouldn't wake up. She wanted them with her just as much as they wanted to be there.

Gail smiled as she curled around Travis with Benton at her back. Spring had brought a lot to them, but most importantly, it had brought them Grace and sealed them as a family once and for all.

THE END

WWW.MARLAMONROE.COM

Siren Publishing, Inc.
www.SirenPublishing.com

CPSIA information can be obtained
at www.ICGtesting.com
Printed in the USA
LVOW10s1446100418

572940LV00030B/773/P